D0231824

Rogue's Gallery

By Robert Barnard

Sheer Torture
The Mistress of Alderley
A Cry from the Dark
The Graveyard Position
Dying Flames
A Fall from Grace
Last Post
The Killings on Jubilee Terrace
A Stranger in the Family
A Mansion and its Murder
Rogue's Gallery (a short story collection)

a&b

Rogue's Gallery

ROBERT BARNARD

First published in Great Britain in 2011 by
Allison & Busby Limited
13 Charlotte Mews
London W1T 4EJ
www.allisonandbusby.com

A CIP catalogue record for this book is available from
the British Library.

10 9 8 7 6 5 4 3 2 1

ISBN 978-0-7490-1017-1

Typeset in 11/16.5 pt Sabon by
Allison & Busby Ltd.

Paper used in this publication is from sustainably managed sources.
All of the wood used is procured from legal sources and is fully traceable.
The producing mill uses schemes such as ISO 14001
to monitor environmental impact.

Printed and bound by
CPI Group (UK) Ltd, Croydon, CR0 4YY

ROGUE'S GALLERY

Contents

Rogue's Gallery

When the Gallery of the Palazzo Cenci-Corombona was about to be opened for the first time to the public there was a private viewing in advance of opening for art critics and newspaper columnists, and a further one two days later for princes, dukes, counts and the assorted riff-raff of Roman society. On the first of these days the critics strolled around the high and densely-packed rooms and galleries, sniffing a little at the dim Teniers landscapes, raising an eyebrow at allegorical nothings by Angelica Kauffman, wondering whether the rubric under the Caravaggio shouldn't have read 'School of', and generally being interested rather than impressed.

Antonio Scaltri ('Toni' to his friends), the art critic of the *Corriere della Mattina,* went round rather more quickly than most, because he'd given the collection the once-over at a party two or three years before. It was only when he came to a little alcove with a curtain across the entrance and the legend 'Van Dyck Room' above it that his interest was quickened. He did not remember a Van Dyck in the collection. As he reached to draw aside the curtain a light automatically came on in the little side-room, and he registered that there was only one picture, and turned to look at it. For some seconds he was speechless.

'*Dio mio*!' he said at last. Then, since he was an international expert on seventeenth-century portraiture, known in five continents, he added in English: 'Wow!'

The idea of opening up the gallery wing of the palazzo had come to Prince Paolo, or been fed to him, one day after lunch, when his wife had driven off in her new Smart car, which parked in half the space of a normal car and cost decidedly more than one – ideal for her afternoon round of visits to her smart middle-aged friends to talk about ancestry and clothes, and to the current smart boutique to do the same. The son and heir was out with his younger smart friends, speeding around the town high on heroin or alcohol, and probably with the current bimbo to whom the prince so strongly objected, though when it came to brains most people would feel that she and the young heir were ideally suited.

So the prince could meditate on his financial predicament.

The Cenci-Corombonas were only a distant branch of the great Cenci line, but like them they believed in keeping things within the family. In their case this meant hoarding their wealth, adding to it in safe, traditional ways, and handing status and loot on unimpaired from one generation to the next. They delighted in profitable, risk-free positions such as the prince's own Vice-Chairmanship of the Banco dei Ladri Siciliani. This policy, however, had been subtly changed in the last twenty years by Prince Paolo. Where his ancestors had despised the Stock Exchange as being full of dubious characters of low birth and hare-brained projects, the prince had decided that it was the only way for a wealthy family to prosper in the modern world. Unfortunately he had entered into this new world with more enthusiasm than flair. He had invested a great deal of money into Microsoft companies that were all prospectus and no funds, and into the firms created by the privatisation of the British railways, having always been an Anglophile by inclination. It was two weeks after the declared bankruptcy of Railtrack that the prince sat at table, with coffee and brandy, and entertained thoughts of the most gloomy.

'If I sell a picture,' he said to Silvio, his butler, with whom he had, in truth, more in common than with any of his family, 'it will have to be a good one.'

'That would be sad, sir,' murmured Silvio.

'Sell one of the lesser ones and it would only bring in a few million lire. Tide me over for a few months and that would be all.'

'On the other hand, sell one of the good ones, sir, and it would make the collection much less interesting were you ever to decide to open it to the paying public,' said Silvio, making a judicious exit.

The prince's mind ticked over slowly, but a minute or two later he said aloud:

'What a peach of an idea!'

He could open the gallery separately, so there would be no vulgar intrusion on the family part of the palace, and he would charge twelve or fifteen thousand lire admission (what would that be in Euros?), and prepare a lavish and glossy guidebook himself, free of the doubts and condescensions of the professional art historians. The Doria Pamphilj family had been doing it for years, and the tourists flocked to their undesirably-placed palace at the bottom of the Via del Corso. Opening a gallery would mean that he could keep all his pictures and create a regular and continuing source of income. It was a brilliant, brilliant idea!

It was characteristic of the prince, who was not optimistic by nature except in his gambling and his share dealings, that by the time Silvio returned for the coffee cups, he had spotted a snag.

'That idea about opening the gallery to the public,' he said.

'Sir?'

'The Doria Pamphilj do, and they pull in the masses. But they've got one marvellous picture.'

'The Velasquez of Innocent X, sir. Quite.'

'That's it. I knew you'd remember. One of the greatest portraits ever painted, they say, and popularised by that English johnny.'

'Bacon, sir. Francis Bacon.'

'I knew the name was familiar. Well, the truth is, good though our collection is, we haven't got anything of absolutely first-class standard. Not anything that would stand out and bring in the hoi polloi.'

Silvio coughed.

'Aren't you forgetting the Van Dyck, sir?'

Since in fiction only brilliant ideas, rather unrealistically, seem to emanate from butlers, it is only fair (since the prince in the preparations for opening always referred to the idea as his own) to underline that it was the butler of the Palazzo Cenci-Corombona who bore the responsibility for originating this particular brilliant wheeze.

The suggestion of Silvio certainly presented the prince with problems, both of a familial and a practical nature: would the exhibition of that particular picture, remarkable though it was, rebound to the credit of the family, or – more importantly – attract visitors to the gallery?

The elevation of Cardinal Aldo Cenci-Corombona to the papacy in 1623 represented a distinct deviation from the family's traditional avoidance of positions of prominence that demanded integrity, public scrutiny or hard work. His surprising promotion arose from a situation familiar to those choosing the winner of the Booker Prize or the next leader of the Conservative Party. In the Conclave to choose a successor to Pope Gregory XV there were two brilliant candidates, both with roughly equal support: there was the Cardinal-Archbishop of Pistoia, a man of notable piety who had very little control over his lawless flock, and there was Cardinal Salvini, a member of the Vatican's administrative hierarchy, who had a genius for organisation extending from the high ground of strategy and policy to the low ground of who cooked the papal polenta, but who was someone who never let 'that religious nonsense' interfere with his grand or his little schemes. These two candidates dominated the first six attempts to select a new pontiff, and as the crowds in St Peter's Square waited in vain for the puff of smoke that would give them the news that a new pope had been chosen, the cardinals sweated for three weeks of a Roman summer, quarrelled among themselves, missed their mistresses and got shorter and shorter tempered. One died, another lost whatever reason he had ever had. A compromise candidate had to be found. That candidate was Cardinal Cenci-Corombona of Naples.

That much might be found in any official account of that particular papal election. What it would probably not include were the rumours. These told that Cardinal Cenci-Corombona, immediately on the death of Gregory XV, had made a very shrewd assessment of who the leading candidates would be and their probable level of support. In the world of today he would have made a superb bookmaker of a rather dodgy kind. Foreseeing a likely stalemate he had told all and sundry that his doctor had diagnosed him as suffering from the wasting disease of phthisis, and had given him only six months to live. Six months! That suited the two supporters of the other two candidates down to the ground. The College of Cardinals was elderly (apart from the scapegrace 'nephews' of the two previous popes), and numbers could change dramatically in six months.

So, as a compromise candidate, the cardinal was elected Supreme Pontiff, and reigned as Julius IV for the next nineteen years.

It was in the year after his election, 1624, that the new pope was painted by the rising star of Flemish painting, then on a long-term stay in Italy. Van Dyck was gentle, retiring and notably sitter-friendly, softening ugliness to mere ordinariness, reducing obvious villainy to mere worldliness. With all his enthusiasm and hopefulness the young painter was bemused as to how to paint the new pontiff. Julius was small, twisted in body, unprepossessing to the nth degree. But pity can be aroused for an unsightly exterior. What made the problems of presentation almost insurmountable was the face; mean, beetle-browed, gnarled into a perennial expression of rage and loathing that directed itself on his interlocutors – and hence on the painter of his portrait – with terrifying force and intensity. Van Dyck confessed himself beaten.

'I try,' he confessed to his Flemish friends at the inn off the Piazza Navona where they met at nights. 'I try so hard – to give him dignity, benignity, even pathos. Nothing will help. Something – I don't know what – keeps breaking through.'

'I think it's called Evil,' said his friend Sustermanns.

Certainly Van Dyck took the finished painting to the Vatican with no high hopes. He shivered as he removed the covering veil. The new pope was outraged, incandescent. After ten minutes of rant he had the upstart painter kicked out as unceremoniously as that other upstart Mozart was later to be by the Archbishop of Salzburg.

Nourishing his hurt and his grievance, Van Dyck returned to his home base in Genoa, where he worked night and day for three weeks on the picture, removing all the softening effects he had vainly tried to introduce, attempting finally to capture the atmosphere of brutal malignity which the pope communicated to all who came into contact with him.

When he had achieved to his own satisfaction a version which captured the hellish horror of the man, he offered it to the Cardinal-Archbishop of Pistoia, the new pope's saintly rival, who accepted it with alacrity.

'I need to be reminded,' he said via his envoy, 'that Satan does indeed walk among us.'

It was from descendants of that man's brother that the Cenci-Corombonas bought the picture in the early 1700s, immediately putting it in store in an inaccessible part of their cellar. They had no desire to remind Romans of the pontificate of Julius IV, and were glad to prevent anyone else doing so.

It was in that same inaccessible cellar that Prince Paolo, accompanied by Silvio, had viewed the picture soon after he became head of the family in 1978. It was from there that they removed it when the time came to open the gallery to the public in 2001.

'*Dio mio*!' said Toni Scaltri of the *Corriere della Mattina*. 'Wow!'

The man in the picture that overwhelmed him had all the trappings of the papacy as assuredly as Innocent X did in the famous portrait by Velazquez that the prince had alluded to: the purple-red of the vestments and *biretta*, the throne-like chair, the *mozzetta*, and the token sign of piety too – in Julius's case, a prayer book in his right hand. But the trappings could only serve to highlight the face: topping the hunched-forward body it thrust itself at you, seeming to deliver a rebuke at you – no, not a rebuke, Toni decided, but a string of vituperative obscenities from that twisted mouth, beneath that flaring nose and that mean, grasping, low brow. But that inventory missed out on the eyes. Through the grime of centuries – for Silvio had wisely advised against cleaning the picture, feeling the force of it would be more generally acceptable from appearing beneath a veneer of dirt – they still seemed to consume both themselves and the viewer with their flaming rage and hatred. Satan indeed, said Toni to himself, unconsciously echoing the Archbishop's words: Satan viewing the world's last vestiges of goodness and piety with outrage, and issuing a strident proclamation of war.

For five minutes Toni stood alone before this great unseen portrait of his chosen century. Then he staggered back to his fellow critics and newsmen, feeling weakened by the experience. Confronting their polite indifference to the body of the collection, Toni had difficulty finding appropriate words.

'Wait till you see the Van Dyck,' he warned them. 'It's . . . tremendous . . . too much . . . too horrible.'

Something similar was said two nights later at the special society viewing by Paolo's wife, Princess Francesca, who looked into the room with her friend the Countess Malatesta, glanced at the picture, then looked hurriedly away.

'Too ghastly, my dear,' she muttered to her friend. 'Just too hideously ugly. But you wouldn't expect looks or style from a pope, would you? Especially not a Cenci-Corombona one.'

For the princess was born a Strozzi, and had nothing but contempt for the parvenu branch (four and a half centuries) of the family she had lowered herself into by marriage. Her friend gazed at the picture for a minute as if mesmerised, then dragged her eyes away with a harsh laugh.

'He looks like a dustman dressed up for carnival,' she said.

The two preliminary viewings certainly paid off. The news of an extraordinary picture of an ancestor of the Cenci-Corombonas filtered down from the society guests as wealth is supposed to but seldom does. The critics sent out a great buzz of interest, and Toni Scaltri, feeling the need as the greatest expert in the field to absorb the experience before writing about it, postponed coming to terms with this unexpected side to the gentle and pliable Flemish master by adding a final note to his fortnightly piece urging readers to go hotfoot to the Palazzo and view the extraordinary new picture which had previously been kept exclusively within the family. 'See it, see it, see it,' he urged, promising to return to the subject at length in his next article.

The results of this interest were very gratifying. From the moment the doors opened there was a constant trickle of visitors, which augmented itself into a minor stream when the tour guides realised they had a new and extraordinary experience to offer their more discriminating parties. The prince hovered around on the gallery's outskirts, watching who bought the new glossy guide, which firms brought the best-dressed American and Japanese parties, who talked most discerningly about the collection. In the early days he dressed very casually, hoping to be mistaken for a workman, but as the success of the enterprise became obvious he resumed his English tweeds (for winter was drawing on) and started thinking of himself as a man of some importance in Rome. None of his family had been that since Prince Marcello in the mid-nineteenth century, who had been in the party that welcomed to the city Vittorio Emanuele II as the new King of Italy and had become his first interpreter, translating his guttural Savoyard dialect pronouncements into an Italian the Romans could understand, then going on to pimp for his son Umberto I, a job that gave him greater aesthetic satisfaction but which finally had to be given up when the workload proved too great. Now the family had another man of influence at its head.

Unfortunately Toni Scaltri's article never got finished. He suffered a massive heart attack just when he was approaching its peroration. His newspaper, however, somewhat ghoulishly published the piece 'just as he left it', thus allowing their readers to share Toni's last thoughts on one of the great figures of his chosen century:

> *'It is as if this mild-mannered, ingratiating young man from Antwerp had, thus early in his career, an experience that rid him of all anger, all bile – as if he painted out of himself in this one picture all urge to be totally honest about his subjects, just by reason of the fact that he, for this once only, had captured a true monster in all his hideous monstrosity. This extraordinary pic—'*

'It is at this point,' said the *Corriere della Mattina*, adapting the words of Toscanini on the first night of *Turandot*, 'that the Master laid down his pen'. The article created a still greater furore by reason of its macabre unfinished state.

Princess Francesca played little part in the early success of the new gallery. Her friend the Countess Malatesta was stricken with a terrible illness which her doctors pronounced on most learnedly to conceal their total mystification. As she began at last to recover they prescribed a lengthy stay away in the warm south of the country, to avoid the nip of a Roman winter. The princess was desolated by her loss.

'Apparently she just lay there,' she told her husband, watching his face closely, 'and all she said was "The eyes, the eyes."'

Her husband, from long practice, kept his face totally impassive. He had heard a day or two before that an American party had suffered no less than two deaths in the days after their visit to the Gallery Cenci-Corombona. By chance he had observed this particular party, and had estimated the average weight of its members to be around twenty stone. He had amused himself by wondering about the economics of hiring a forty-seater coach that could only accommodate twenty posteriors. He wasn't surprised at two heart attacks occurring to greatly overweight people in the stressful environment of Rome, but he expressed his princely sympathy to the company, as he did to the relatives of an elderly Swedish lady who had gone off her head the day after her visit. He did wonder why he had been informed of these unfortunate occurrences, and it did not occur to him that people were playing around with the idea of suing for compensation.

Because talk was getting around. The ridiculous words

'evil eye' were gaining currency. In the wake of talk about deaths and near-deaths there came talk about the picture: nonsense about people who had seen it bathed in a hellish red light, about terrible eyes that seemed to spew sparks, more tales about disaster occurring to those who had gazed too long or commented too scathingly on the subject. Some such as Silvio, who saw the painting often in the course of their duty, felt that some process of internal heat was burning away the dirt of centuries, to reveal the blazing eyes as more terrible each day. The talk even got into the popular press. '*It is as if the evil spirit of the painting, dampened by centuries, gathering dust in a cellar, has gradually reawakened, has flexed its diabolical muscles, and is now wreaking vengeance on the unfortunate visitors to the Gallery Cenci-Corombona*,' said one daily paper too low to be taken at the Palazzo, but seen by Silvio.

That piece alone was enough to scare the tour operators. Americans are the most timorous tribe on earth and, after the Italians, the most superstitious. The numbers on the pre-booked tours dwindled, as many chose to go shopping on the Via Veneto instead. Then tours were cancelled altogether, with no reason given. Casual Italian visitors now passed the doorway of the palace with a boding shake of the head. Silvio, anguished by self-blame, joined his master in watching the daily comings and goings in the gallery, and listening to the comments. So few were coming that it would soon cease to be a viable concern. Those that did come viewed the dim and dusty body of the collection, but when they came to the Van Dyck Room they sped by it. 'You wouldn't catch me going in there,' they heard one English visitor say. Another claimed to have seen a terrible light penetrating even the thick velvet curtains, and had heard supernatural music.

'I'm afraid, sir,' Silvio said *sotto voce* one day to his master, as they stood in the long gallery that ended in the Van Dyck Room, 'that the experiment is running into difficulties.'

'Nonsense,' said the prince, though the heartiness in his voice rang false. 'It's just that the novelty has worn off for the moment. The numbers will pick up again.'

'It's the recent publicity,' insisted Silvio. 'People don't forget that kind of thing. I don't see the numbers ever recovering from the stories of people dying after coming here.'

'Pooh, pooh! It will take more than the nonsense in the Rome scandal sheets to destroy this gallery. Their sensations are five-day ones. They will soon be forgotten and people will start streaming back.'

'Nevertheless, I wonder whether we should continue to show the Van Dyck.'

'But the collection is nothing without that – at least not specially remarkable,' amended the prince hurriedly. 'Showing the Pope Julius was a brilliant suggestion on your part.'

It was the first time Silvio had heard his own part in the creation of the gallery acknowledged – when failure was staring them in the face. It irked him.

'Nevertheless, I notice that you don't go and view the picture, sir,' he said.

'Why would I? That ugly old scamp means less than nothing to me. Why should I ruin my digestion looking at him?' Silvio remained silent. The prince, rightly, thought he was being challenged. 'Oh well, if you think it would restore confidence.'

Squaring his shoulders, without so much as a glance at his fairly loyal butler, Prince Paolo set his long, tweed-clad legs in motion and, watched by the little knots of visitors to the gallery, strode past his Teniers and his Sustermanns, further, further down the long room until, unlucky gambler to the last, he pulled aside the heavy curtain and entered the brightly-lit alcove.

The New Slavery

It had all started so innocently.

'Dad, could you do me a favour?'

Terence Munday regarded his daughter-in-law. Her plump, squat body always reminded him of an over-full plastic shopping bag.

'Of course, Gloria, if I can.'

'It's the next two weeks. My boss is away, and all his work is landed on me. I'll have to go in one hour early, just to keep my head above water.'

'You want me to take the children to school and collect them in the afternoon.'

'That's right, Dad. You can drive them straight home and leave them there. They quite like being their own bosses, and Victoria is very good at sorting out any problems.'

Terence kept shtum on whether he would leave the children to their own devices at their home or bring them there to his own semi in one of the western suburbs of Leeds.

'I can manage quite well for a fortnight,' he said. 'I think I'll enjoy it.'

And enjoy it he did. He had always liked the three children and he wished that Gloria and his son Martin showed more evidence of loving them, or of having wanted them in the first place. Having them in his own house without their parents to shout do's and don't's at them was a little fountain of pleasures and satisfactions. He resurrected old games that Martin and his sister Joy had played as children, he dusted down jigsaws, tried to digest the rules of Cluedo and Totopoly and bought drinks, biscuits and cakes he knew they liked.

'Bags I sit beside grandad,' said Victoria, aged eight, and conscious that she was a favourite. 'He finds it difficult to master the rules.'

'Cheeky brat,' said Terence, loving it.

Larry was seven: he had been born to complete the family, and he was almost as bright and on the ball as Victoria. Marcus was four, was always announced as an accident, but had never managed to sort out in his mind traffic, air or railway train, the only things he had ever heard paired with the word accident. Terence loved him with a trace of pity for the weakest branch. The children were good friends with each other, but Terence never took them home and left them there. He knew that if he got there at six-thirty Gloria would arrive back within a few minutes, and he stayed there until she did. She made no comment on this, and certainly did not regard it as a criticism of her own lower standards. Terence had to admit that his son Martin was a policeman whose hours of work were horribly irregular – a fact which did not make things easy for the household.

When the two weeks were up, nothing was said. After he had been going through the routine of collecting them from home at eight-thirty, driving them to school, then meeting them out of school at three-twenty, driving them to his home, feeding them and playing with them, then driving them to their own home, Gloria did say the odd words of thanks such as 'You're a brick,' or 'I don't know what I'd do without you,' but she never put any warmth into the words, and she never suggested payment for his services, though he knew she earned many times his pension from the local authority which had employed him as a gardener. The assumption seemed to be that these services were given with love and paid with the same coinage. Terence did once hear, through an open kitchen window, Gloria say to a neighbour 'I wouldn't insult him by suggesting it.' He decided he wouldn't have accepted any offer, but he wouldn't have been insulted by it either.

Though Terence did not measure his services to his family in monetary terms it was inevitable that now and then the question of money would come up. When Victoria complained that her school blouse was getting tight and there were holes in her school socks, Terence took her after school to the shops in Pudsey that stocked them and bought a blouse and two pairs of socks. When Gloria came home that evening he said:

'Oh, Victoria needed a new blouse and one or two things. I've kept the receipt.'

He handed the scrap of paper over, and Gloria grabbed

it on her way to the kitchen. She crumpled it up, and Terence suspected that she threw it straight into the bin under the sink. He never brought the subject up again, but from then on he had to force himself to speak respectfully to his daughter-in-law, or even keep up a friendly tone.

Some nights when he was not too tired he tried to put together a summary of how much being *au pair* to the little family cost him. He took all his supermarket checkout slips and noted down all the food items bought for the family or shared by them. He noted down petrol, then roughly how much their share in any little treats cost him. Then he found a figure for the heating of the house, and made a guess at their share in the water rate.

He never even thought of handing Gloria a bill. In fact he never completed the complicated sum. He worked off something by trying to come to an estimate, but it made him feel too mean. He couldn't calculate how much looking after the grandchildren cost him because he could never cost the other side of the equation – the joy that having the children with him brought to him, the pride that he took in their successes in exams and in games and PT at school.

He soon had an addition to his little family. His daughter Joy was married to a teacher, and though his hours made this a convenience there were times when his job took him out for an evening, and Joy as well. There was between Joy and Gloria an edgy state of near-open warfare, and Joy told her husband she didn't see why she should pay for babysitters on social occasions when she knew Gloria and Martin got their father's services for free. She brought it up with Terence, and he told her he could well manage little

William for a few hours after school, but he needed the later hours in the evening to recuperate after looking after the children for three or four hours a day.

'I'm not as young as I was,' he said.

'Of course, Dad,' said Joy. 'I meant after school.'

So William joined his cousins now and then, and Terence welcomed the chance to get to know him better. Quite soon Joy forgot about his need to have his evenings to himself, and Terence didn't like to mention it, because, as he told his friends in the King's Arms, it was only now and then. There never was a slave who cooperated more willingly in his enslavement.

The children of course talked. All children talk, except the seriously abused.

'Mummy slapped Marcus last night,' said Larry.

'I expect he richly deserved it,' said Terence.

Terence was always careful never to let a word of criticism of Gloria cross his lips. He was of a generation that did not regard a slap as 'violence'. He never mentioned it to her, or treated such an event as anything other than normal behaviour in families.

'Daddy didn't come home last night,' said Victoria, as they were getting ready to go home one evening.

'Policemen's hours are cruel,' said Terence. 'They do an awful lot of overtime if they've got a difficult case on. It's rotten for the families.'

'Yes, but—' began Victoria.

'Well, my darling?'

'Oh nothing.'

It was three days later that Terence, making sure his

voice was casual, entirely non-inquisitorial, asked: 'Is your Daddy still very busy?' The children looked at one another.

'Yes,' said Victoria. Then, after a long silence, she said: 'Mummy says she doesn't know when he'll be back.'

'Oh dear.' Terence found he did not know what line to take, so it just came out as: 'You know you've always got me.'

'Yes,' said Larry. 'And we could always come and live here, couldn't we?'

'Of course you could,' said Terence.

He was conscious of Victoria wanting to say something and feared it was some comment on his age. So he said: 'Let's not say anything about this now. And *please* all of you, don't say anything about it at home. So far as we're concerned, I know nothing about it. Much better that way. It's probably that your Dad is just having a brief fling, and he'll come to his senses.'

'What is a fling?' asked Marcus. As so often he was ignored.

As it turned out Terence was underestimating Gloria, as one often does people one doesn't like. Gloria realised perfectly well that the children would have talked to their grandfather about the disappearance of his son. She arrived one afternoon with a couple of suitcases of clothing.

'Dad – you're going to have to have the children for a few days. I can't let this business with Martin go on any longer. I've got to find something to do about it. Either he's the father of this family, and comes home to them in the few hours a day he can call his own, or he has gone off permanently with this floozie he's taken up with.'

Terence led her off to the kitchen. 'So he's not come back. Has he written? Phoned?'

'Not a thing. Of course I've known about the floozie for months.'

'You managed not to reveal it. I had no idea before I talked about it with the children.'

'Well, you know I never want to upset you. There's plenty of changes of clothes in the suitcases, and most of the things don't need to be ironed. It's best there are as few changes as possible. The children don't like being talked about at school, and I'd certainly prefer it that way. Bye Dad.'

So from then on Terence was on his own. He already had the key to the children's home, so he could go there for any clothing, game or toy that one or other of the children might want. When they went round, the children looked at the rooms as if they found it odd that nothing had changed from visit to visit. Their relief at closing the door on the place was obvious.

Terence tried to keep a balance in all things. If he brought home a bright pair of socks for one of them, he was careful to provide a comparable treat for the other two. The children at school never noticed any change in the Munday children, so there were no explanations to upset them.

When Marcus reached five, a five-pound note came in the post with a postcard from the bottom drawer with 'Love, your Mum' scrawled on the back and a cosy kitten on the front. Marcus was at this time into animals.

'You're like me,' said Terence. 'I used to love animals,

though it was wartime, and there weren't many toys to be bought.'

'What did you like best?' demanded Marcus.

'My kangaroo. He was called Kanga, or Jackie. I loved him, and I cried blue murder if he went missing.'

'What is blue murder?'

'A big fuss,' said Terence, who made a mental resolution to avoid such words in future.

'Can I have a kangaroo too?'

'If we searched around in the attic we could probably find old Jackie. Then we could get you something else.'

'Yes! He'll need a lot of loving if he's been up in the attic for ages and ages.'

So they found the brown knitted kangaroo, and the five-pound note went towards a panda, who was loved but not as Jackie was loved. Terence decided Jackie got the residue of love that Marcus found it difficult or confusing to express to his grandfather.

The next birthday was Victoria's. Nothing came on the day, or for more than a week afterwards, but then a real birthday card came, with a ten-pound note and 'Thanks for all you're doing Dad' on the inside. 'It's really for you, grandad,' said Victoria, quite without grievance or rancour. The last card to come had coincidentally a kangaroo on it. It came from Gloria who was in Australia, but she was a month out for Terence's birthday.

By now the children were entirely settled with their grandfather. So confident and happy were they that Terence wished his wife was still alive, so she could see. She had loved Martin and Joy, but she had sometimes shook her head and said: 'They're all for number one, both of them.' Terence would have liked to have introduced her to their grandchildren and proved that a rather dubious inheritance from the parents need not signify an unhappy and self-obsessed future. He loved the way the quartet (because William came round more and more, having no companions at home) absorbed all his teachings (because Terence was a born teacher, skilled in disguising what was taught with a spoonful of sugar). When they were all out together they often met friends and very kindly involved him in conversation and activities. 'This is our grandad,' one of them would say. Later it was 'This is our grandad – he is looking after us', and later still it was 'This is our grandad – he looks after us' and he knew that if they had mapped out a future in their minds, it put him always in the position of parent. It warmed him, but still he worried a bit about it too.

One day when they were all at school he decided he ought to do something about the children's father. He had heard nothing at all from him for the eight months he had been looking after them. He decided to ring up Martin's last permanent police station.

'Could I speak to Martin Munday please?'

'Who?'

'Martin Munday. He was attached to you last year I know.'

'Oh, Munday. Yes, of course. I'll put you through to Inspector Platt.' Inspector Platt was audibly embarrassed. He asked Terence to come round to the station.

'Look,' said Terence. 'I don't need to be handled with

kid gloves. Martin's my son, and I know he's not perfect. I'm seventy-two but I'm perfectly healthy, and I have three children to look after. My day is pretty busy, and I'd be obliged if you would do this on the phone.'

'Yes . . . right . . . well – Martin is currently under suspension. He first came to our attention at the time of his separation from his wife.'

'Is that what it was?'

'At that time. And the detective squad at Halifax where he was stationed was investigating a crime gang in that town that had links with a really big and nasty Manchester gang. We think your son took over the leader's mistress when she was becoming more trouble than she was worth to the gang. We think he leaked police plans and information, then began to forge links with other gangs. That's when we moved in and suspended him. It got into the Manchester papers, but nowhere else. I'm sorry you had to hear it like this.'

'So am I.'

'You've got the children, haven't you?'

'I have. Thank God.'

'Keep them away from your son.'

And he did that, insofar as he needed to. Martin, Inspector Platt told him, had almost certainly moved to Manchester, was not cooperating with the police investigation, and was almost sure to be sacked. Terence did not need to be a mother hen. Martin would have no use for his offspring.

It was now, he realised, that his feelings for the children underwent a change. He had always loved them as grandparents do – with the addition of a scintilla of grudge that he had been handed them without so much as a 'by your leave'. Now the love he felt for them had become overwhelming – the love of his life, eclipsing all thought of his own children, all memories of his own wife. They were his, his alone. They were wonderful kids, doing just what he had trained them to do, helping around the house, helping each other, their brains (even Marcus's lately) sharp as scissors, and retaining a remarkable amount of information and comment. They were his offspring, pure and simple, and he blessed a God he had up to now barely believed in for his good fortune.

Holidays were the best times of all. He could be with them all the time, apart from some token hours spent with their school friends. They would play a slimmed down form of cricket in Kirkstall Abbey Park, and when it rained they played Monopoly or whist, and he began teaching Victoria chess.

They were still children, not prodigies. They loved going to shopping centres, or the Victoria Quarter in Leeds. They had children's love of colour and mechanical toys. Out at the White Rose Centre they went mad in shop after shop, though to Terence's eyes they had just the same merchandise in the smaller branches in central Leeds. They each had a sum to spend that depended on their ages. They always consulted with him about what they were going to buy, except when it was sweets, a subject on which they consulted their own preferences. Larry was clutching a bag of liquorice torpedos one day in the White Rose Centre, when only the three were with him, when suddenly he stopped in his tracks.

'Daddy! Daddy!'

Something in Terence seemed to stop. A flick of the heart seemed to touch him and run through him, like the touch of a fern or a flower at a crowded wedding. He saw the three children run towards a flashy man, saw him draw to him a ridiculously flashy woman, then saw him as the children drew themselves up, smiling and laughing, and Terence heard his son, retreating hurriedly, say: 'Sorry, kids. You've got the wrong man.'

Then suddenly a real pain struck – sudden, cruel, incredibly sharp. He staggered down on to his knees, and as he forced open his eyes he saw the three children looking at him. In their eyes he saw love and pity, but he saw also fear – a terror at what could await them, rejected as they were by both parents, and now left alone by the one person they worshipped for his generous, unwise love.

Sins Of Scarlet

Cardinal Pascona stood a little aside from his fellow electors, observing the scene, conjecturing on the conversations that were animating every little knot of cardinals. The elderly men predominated, of course. The young men were not only in a minority, but they were unlikely to want any of their number to be elected. A long papacy was the last thing anybody wanted at this juncture. So instead of forming up into a clique of their own, they separated and mingled with the older men. They were all, in any case, related in some way or other to earlier popes, and their opinions for that reason tended to be discounted. That was unfair but understandable.

Cardinal Borromei.

That was the name that kept coming towards him, through the sticky and fetid air of the chapel. It was clear to Pascona that opinion was drifting – had already drifted – in that direction. Borromei was related to a previous pope, like the young men, but his promotion to the rank of cardinal at the age of twenty-three was now so long ago that everybody had discounted it. He had proved his worth to the college by a long life of steady opinions, safe hands on the tiller, and general mediocrity. He was a man to ruffle no feathers, stir up no hornet's nests, raise no high winds.

Ideal.

Or ideal in the view of most of his fellow electors. And promising in other ways too: aged sixty-seven and obese from a fondness for rich and outré foods. That, and a partiality for the finest cognac, marked him out as likely to be present before long in the chapel in mummified form only. Cardinal Pascona stepped down from the chapel stalls and began mingling with the knots of his fellows. The conversations were going as he had expected.

'The situation in France is becoming worrying,' that old fool da Ponti was saying to a little group of like-minded ciphers. 'Borromei has been used to a mediation role in Venice. Couldn't be bettered at the present time.' He turned with mischievous intent to Pascona. 'Wouldn't you agree?' He continued looking at him, and Pascona knew that any dissent would be discounted as the bile of an unsuccessful candidate. Everyone in the conclave assessed Pascona as *papabile* but there was a distinct reluctance to vote for him.

'Absolutely,' Pascona said with a smile. 'A perfectly safe pair of hands, and accustomed to bringing peace to warring factions.' He could not restrain himself from adding: 'Though whether the Bourbons – fairweather friends to us, at their best – deserve the services of the Church's best mediator is another matter. The unkind might suggest that they deserve to stew in a juice of their own making.'

And he moved on, with a peaceful, delightful glide as if, having just dispensed a Christlike wisdom, he was currently walking on air.

The bowls from their light supper were just being cleared away. Pascona nodded in the direction of the robed and cowled figures who silently served them and waited for them to bring the silver goblets with their nightcaps in them. A vile red wine from Sicily in all probability. It was generally agreed among the cardinals that everything was done to make their stay incommunicado from the real world (if Rome and the Vatican was that) as unpleasant as possible. The aim of the Vatican officials was to persuade them to make a decision as quickly as they reasonably could so that a return to normality could be achieved. After all, for those officials, it was only a matter of one old man being succeeded by another old man. Nothing much happened during the last reign, and (unless a surprising choice was made) nothing much would happen in the next one.

Cardinal Pascona took up his goblet. It was indeed a vile wine, quite incredibly sour and thick. Prolonged indigestion or worse could well be the consequences for many of the elderly and infirm electors if they did more than sip at such muck. Confident in his own stomach, the cardinal drank, then went over to another group.

'It is a sobering thought,' he injected into their small talk that was by now a mere prelude to slumber, 'that the world is waiting on our decision, but when the choice is announced everyone will say "Who?"'

The cardinals smiled politely, though one or two of the smiles were sour. Not all of them liked to be thought totally insignificant in the wider scheme of things. Now the cowled figures were going round extinguishing the nests of candles on the walls. They rolled out the down mattresses and put on top of them a pillow and a pile of blankets hardly needed in the close atmosphere of the Sistine. Beside these bundles they put a nightlight. No great comforts for a long night. Cardinals removed their red robes and lay down in their substantial undergarments. Bones creaked as they levered themselves down. Cardinal Pascona took great care not to creak himself. He was still fit and active in every way. That ought to be noticed. He was not going to live for ever, but he had a few years yet in him, and good ones too.

He lay on his back looking up. Nothing could be seen of the ceiling, but in the murky light cast by the few remaining nightlights he could distinguish the contours of the chapel. He had loved the chapel since he had first seen it, fifty years before. It spoke to him. Twenty years before, when he was barely forty, he had become part of a commission to report on the state of the chapel, in particular on the state of Mazzuoli's restorations at the beginning of the century. Pascona had sat on the scaffolding day after day, eventually dressing as a workman, sharing their bread and wine, getting to *know* every inch of the ceiling and the altar wall and the *Last Judgment* fresco. The commission had reported, but nothing had been done. Business as usual at the Vatican!

He altered the position of his bed so that his head was towards the altar. He did not want to think of the *Last Judgment*. Fine, terrifying, but the Christ was not his Christ – too commanding, too much an obvious man of action.

A general, an organiser, that was Michelangelo's Christ. Whereas his was gentler, more of a healer, more forgiving. He would be forgiving, surely?

He lay in the darkness, his eyes fixed on the panels he could not see, recreating the scenes he knew so well, that had been imprinted on his soul some twenty years before. The drunken Noah, a rare scene of comedy, and to the right of that panel his favourite of all the *ignudi* – the naked men holding medallions. A boy-man, infinitely inviting, conscious of his own appeal – delightful, inexhaustible.

But then he let his eye sweep across the darkness of the ceiling and fix on the central panel. The masterpiece among masterpieces in his opinion. The moment of creation. And in particular Adam: beautiful, languid before full awakening, holding hope and promise for all those of Cardinal Pascona's tastes. And so like his own beloved Sandro! The yearning face, the beautiful body – it was as if Sandro had been created for him in the likeness of our first father.

He slept.

He awoke next morning to the sounds of disturbance – shouting, choking, vomiting and groans. He leapt from his bed. The chapel was now fully illuminated and he ran to a little group of cardinals in a circle, gazing down in consternation. In the middle of the circle, writhing on the stone floor, lay the obese figure of Cardinal Borromei. Pascona could only make out one word of his cries.

'*Aiudo*!'

He immediately took control.

'Help he must have. Summon a doctor!'

Cardinal da Ponti stepped in with his usual statement of the obvious. 'You know we cannot allow one in. The best we can do is get him out of the chapel to be treated there.'

'And that of course is what we must do.'

'But he should be here. Today might be the day when . . . And it might be just indigestion.'

Cardinal Pascona paused, momentarily uncertain.

'Cardinal Borromei is someone who enjoys the pleasures of the table. But there have been few pleasures of the table on offer here in the chapel. Spartan fare every day so far. The wine last night was disgraceful . . .'

He was about to put aside his indecision and insist that the tormented man be removed and treated outside the chapel when the whole body of cardinals was transfixed by a terrible cry. The flabby body on the floor arched, shuddered, then sank motionless back to the floor.

'*E morto*?' someone whispered.

Dead was certainly what he seemed to be. Cardinal Pascona knelt by the body, felt his chest, then put his face and ear close to his mouth. He shook his head.

'Dead,' he said. 'We must – with the permission of the Cardinal Chamberlain – remove the body. Then we must put out a statement to the waiting crowds. I think it should specify a *colpo di sangue* as the cause of death. A stroke.'

'But it didn't look—'

Cardinal Pascona put up his hand and turned to Cardinal da Ponti. 'I specify that because it is easily understood by the least sophisticated member of the crowd. Everyone there will have had some family member – a grandfather, an uncle – who has died of a stroke. It is a question of getting the message across with the least fuss. If some amendment is needed after the doctors have examined him – so be it. But I do not anticipate any need for it.'

'But a death in conclave – and *such* a death: a man who, if I might put it so, was the *favourite*.'

Cardinal Pascona was brusque in the face of such tastelessness.

'But what could be more likely? A large number of elderly men, shut up together in an unhealthy atmosphere, on a diet which – to put it mildly – is not what they are accustomed to. And the candidate in a state of extreme excitement. It has happened before, and it is a wonder that it hasn't happened more often.'

The thought that there had been a precedent excited them all.

'Oh, *has* it happened?' asked Cardinal Morosi, a new boy of fifty-five.

'Indeed. The procession from the chapel out to the Great Square at the time of Pope Benedict XIV's inauguration was delayed for two hours by one of the cardinals falling dead. Excitement, of course.'

'But then the choice had been made,' muttered Cardinal Morosi. Pascona ignored him. He addressed the whole college, summoned from their beds or from the *prima colazione* by that terrible last cry.

'The need now is to remove, with all appropriate ceremonies and mourning, the deceased brother, and then to continue our deliberations. The whole world awaits our decision. We must not be found wanting at this crisis in our history, and that of the world.'

It struck nobody that for Cardinal Pascona 'the whole world' meant effectively the western half of Europe. They busied themselves, summoned the waiting monks who were clearing away the breakfast things, and had Cardinal Borromei removed from the chapel. Having someone willing and able to take charge enlivened their torpid and ageing intellects, and they settled down to discussions in groups with zest and vigour. What was a death, after all, to men for whom it was only a beginning?

Yet, oddly, the initiative and address of Cardinal Pascona had an effect on the discussion which was the reverse of what might have been expected. Put bluntly (which it never was in this conclave), it might have been summed up in the phrase 'Who does he think he is?' The fact that they were all grateful to him for taking charge, were conscious that he had avoided several hours of indecision and in-fighting, did not stop them asking by what right he had taken control, at that moment of crisis, in the affairs of the Church.

'He takes a great deal too much on himself,' one of them said. And it did his chances no good at all.

For though Pascona was *papabile*, he was not the only one to be so. There had been a minor stir of interest in the early days of the conclave in favour of Cardinal Fosca, Archbishop of Palermo. He was a man who had no enemies, usually spoke sense, and was two or three years on the right side of senility. True, there was one thing against him. This was not the fact that he had something of an obsession about a rag-tag-and-bobtail collection of criminals in his native island. It was the Mafia this, the Mafia that the whole time, as if they were set to take over the world. That the cardinals shrugged off and suffered. But what was really against him in many cardinals' eyes was his height. He was barely five feet tall (or 1.5 metres, as the newfangled notions from France had it). Just to be seen by the crowd he would have to have several cushions on his throne when he went out on the balcony to bless the masses. It was likely to cause ridicule, and the Church was aware, since Voltaire, of how susceptible it was to wit, irony and proletarian laughter.

But suddenly, it seemed, Fosca was a decidedly desirable candidate.

Pascona watched and listened in the course of the day. Ballot succeeded ballot, with nothing so democratic as a declaration of the result. But the word went around: the vote for Fosca was inching up, that for Pascona slowly ebbing away. The cardinal went around, talking to all and sundry with imperturbable urbanity – amiable to all, forswearing all controversy. He was among the first to collect his frugal evening meal. By then his mood was contemplative. He gazed benignly at the monks serving the *stufato,* then looked down in the direction of the cardinal from Palermo. As he helped himself to the rough bread there was the tiniest of nods from one of the cowled heads.

'Dear Michelangelo, help one of your greatest admirers and followers,' he prayed that night on his narrow bed. 'Let the vote go to a follower of yourself, as well as a devout servant of Christ.'

Before he slept his mind went not to the *ignudi*, nor to the awakening Adam in the great central panel, but away from the altar to the expelled Adam as, with Eve, and newly conscious of sin, he began the journey out of Paradise.

He smiled, as thoughts of Sandro and their forthcoming pleasures when they were united again warmed his ageing body.

The morning was not a repeat of the day before.

Over breakfast there was talk, and before long it was time to take the first test of opinion, to find out whether straw should be added to the burning voting slips to make black smoke, or whether it should be omitted, to the great joy of the crowds in St Peter's Square as the white smoke emerged. One cardinal had not risen from his bed, and he was the most important of all. Cardinal da Ponti went to shake him awake, then let out a half-suppressed gasp of dismay. The cardinals, oppressed by fear and horror, went over to the bed.

Cardinal Fosco lay, a scrap of humanity, dead as dead. He looked as if he could be bundled up, wrapped in a newsheet, and put out with the rubbish from the conclave's meals.

'*Dio mio*!'

The reactions were various, but more than one started to say what was on everybody's minds. 'But he too was the—'

This time they hesitated to use the term from horse racing. But one by one, being accustomed to bow to authority, they looked towards the man who, only yesterday, had set the tone and solved the problem of what should be done. Somehow Pascona, with his long experience of curias and conclaves, knew they would do that, and was ready. He cleared his throat.

'Fellow cardinals. Friends,' he began. 'Let us pray for our friend whom God has called to himself. And let us at the same time pray for guidance.' There was a murmur of agreement, along with one or two murmurs of something else. After a minute's silence Cardinal Pascona resumed, adopting his pulpit voice.

'I believe we all know what must be done. I think God has spoken to us, each and every one, at this crisis moment – spoken as God always does speak, through the silent voice of our innermost thoughts.' The cardinals muttered agreement, though most of them had had nothing in the interval for silent prayer that could honestly be called a thought. 'He has told us that what must be thought of first at this most difficult moment is the Church: its good name, its primacy and power, and its mission to bring to God all waverers, all wrong-doers, all schismatics. It is the Church and its God-given mission that must be in the forefront of all our minds.'

There was a more confident buzz of agreement.

'We are in a crisis, as I say, in the history of ours, the one true church. In the world at large doubt, distrust and rebellion seethe, distracting the minds of the unlettered, provoking the discontent of the educated. Ridicule, distrust of long-held beliefs, rebellion against the position of the natural leaders of society – all these evils flourish today, as never before. At such a point any event – even an innocent and natural occurrence such as we witness here' – he gestured towards the human scrap on the bed – 'will be taken up, seized upon as a cause of scandal and concern, distorted and blackened with the ingenuity of the Devil himself, who foments and then leads all such discontents and rebellions. Let us make our minds up, let us make our choice quickly, let us conceal what has happened until such a time as it can be announced and accepted as the natural event which in truth it was.'

This time there was a positively enthusiastic reception for his words.

'Come my friends,' resumed Pascona, delighted at the effect of his words, 'let us get down to business. Let us vote, and let us vote to make a decision, and to present to the world a front of unity and amity. And let us treat our friend here with the respect that a lifetime of faithful service demands. Put a blanket over him.'

It worked like a charm. A blanket was thrown over the body of the dead Cardinal Fosco, leaving his head showing. Not dead, only resting seemed to be the message. The living cardinals proceeded to a vote, and even before the last vote was in and counted it was clear that the straw would no longer be required: the smoke would be pure white.

The excitement was palpable. While they remained cloistered in the chapel the other cardinals thumped Pascona on the shoulder and indulged in such bouts of kiddishness as were possible to a collection of men dominated by the dotards. After five minutes of this, and as the chapel was penetrated by sounds of cheering from crowds in the square, the new pope proceeded to the passageway from the chapel to St Peter's, pausing at the door to look towards the altar and the massive depiction of the Last Judgment behind it. Magnificent, but quite wrong, he thought. And perhaps a silly superstition at that.

Then he proceeded into the upper level of the great church, then along towards the door leading on to the balcony. He stopped before the throne, raised on poles like a sedan chair. He let the leading cardinals, led by the Cardinal Chamberlain and helped by the monks who had serviced the conclave, robe him and bestow on him all the insignia of his new office. He behaved with impeccable graciousness.

'What name has Your Holiness decided to be known by?' asked the Chamberlain. Pascona paused before replying.

'I am conscious of the links of my mother's family to this great, this the greatest, office. The fame of Alexander VI will live forever, but the name is too precious for me, and for the Church, for me to assume it. In truth it would be a burden. I shall leave that sacred name to my ancestor, and I shall take the name of the other pope from her family. I shall be known as Calixtus IV.'

The Chamberlain nodded.

From the square there came sounds. Someone, perched somewhere, with good eyesight, must have been able to see through the open door of the balcony. A whisper, then a shout, had gone round.

'It's the Borgia. The Borgia!'

The fame of his mother's family easily eclipsed that of his father's. The tone of the shouts had fear in it, but also admiration, anticipation. What a time Alexander VI's had been! Bread and circuses, and lots of sex. Calixtus IV smiled to himself, then ascended the throne. As he was about to nod to the four carriers to proceed through the door and on to the balcony, one of the monks came forward with a bag of small coins, to scatter to the crowd below. As he handed the bag to the pope, he raised his head and the cowl slipped back an inch or two. There was the loved face: the languid eyes of Michelangelo's Adam, the expression of newly-awakened sensuality, and underneath the coarse robe the body, every inch of which Calixtus knew so well. He took the bag, and returned his gaze.

'Grazie, Ales-*Sandro.*' he said.

Family Values

It was in June 1948 that Mrs Cynthia Webber and her son Simon came to lodge in the Princes Hotel, Pixton. They were well received by the rest of the guests, all of whom were virtually residents. The country had just suffered one of the worst winters Britain had ever known: months of snow-covered land and roads, which, added to the regime of rationing and shortages that the nation had endured since 1939, brought many to the edge of despair. Most of the residents at the Princes blamed the government for the winter, and for everything else. 'What did we fight the war for?' was a common wail. 'We'd have been better off if we'd lost it.'

What was still called the Princes Hotel was in fact a mere wing of the splendid Edwardian structure that overlooked the town from a vantage point that had once seemed to square with the social status of its guests. It was now run by Mrs Hocking, who was more a housekeeper than a manager. She had been put in mainly to keep the old place open. She didn't want casual guests, which was lucky because few were to be had. She took residents at reasonable rates, commandeered their ration books and used them cunningly, and took the burdens of effort and decision from their shoulders. That was what the middle-aged and elderly residents wanted, particularly after the privations of the terrible winter. And when Mrs Webber and her son arrived they were welcomed as a new source of interest.

'She'll do,' said Major Catchpole, a man of few words.

'Such a *nice* sort of person,' said Mrs Forrest, meaning 'so obviously a gentlewoman.' She added that it was lovely to see a mother and son who were such good friends.

Their arrival had been well signalled in advance because they had taken the suite. All the residents being, by chance or circumstance, single, 'the suite' was the one area in the wing that was not let out. It had been used by families before the war, many of whom came to the Peak District for the sake of a disabled or invalid child, hoping the famous Pixton waters would do them good, if a cure was out of the question. It had two bedrooms with a sitting room between – not large rooms, but providing a degree of comfort and privacy unknown to the other residents. Mrs Hocking, when she had received the enquiry, had been dubious whether the suite was habitable, but with the help of an army of hotel and hospital cleaners, all resident in the town and experienced from the Old Days, the dusty old rooms were smartened up. Even the residents pitched in, with Miss Rumbold volunteering to wash up all the ornaments and crockery in the suite, and old Mr Somervell, a traditional and sentimental soul, buying a bouquet with his own money to decorate the sitting room on the day of their arrival.

They fitted in at once. Mrs Webber, though not unduly confidential, was frank about their situation.

'Simon is going up to Oxford in October. He has a place at Lincoln, to read history. He was found unfit for national service – lungs, you know – but his education was very disturbed in his last years, when the old teachers returned from the war and wanted all the old ways back. He's going to do a very stiff course of reading – the car is full of books – so that he can go up with the best possible basis for study.'

The car was a basis of wonder, Mrs Webber being a widow lady, and she explained it readily.

'It was my husband's car. He died last year – old war wound from the Somme. He was in the Civil Defence, and had an extra petrol ration due to the driving. I've had to give that up, of course, but we just about make do. Simon will take his licence soon.'

Their devotion to each other made Cynthia and Simon objects of great interest to the residents. To play some part in their little personal drama the residents often appealed to them, their judgement and experience seeming to put them on a higher plane than the rest. Simon was appealed to on questions relating to The Younger Generation, Cynthia on matters of fashion, the Royal Family, etiquette, genealogy and even correct English.

'I was always taught at school,' began Mrs Phipps in the manner of all linguistic bores, 'that it should be "ett", the past tense of "eat", not "eight". Don't you agree, Mrs Webber?'

Mrs Webber wiped her mouth with her napkin, perhaps to conceal a smile.

'So often what one was taught at school is either wrong, or has changed with the times. I think either pronunciation is acceptable these days.'

'I happen to know,' said Miss Rumbold, welding together two of the residents' obsessions, 'that the dear Queen says "eight". She visited the British Restaurant in Pimlico when I was doing war work there in 1944. "Eight" she said, definitely.'

'I expect the Queen speaks the language of upper-class Britain a generation or two ago,' said Mrs Webber, who must have been about the same generation as the Queen. 'I know she says "lorss" for "loss", and I think only cockneys and upper-class speakers do that.'

This remark was found daring, but because it was Cynthia it was acceptable.

Mother and son made little excursions in the car on as many afternoons as had sun and as they had petrol for. They didn't ask anyone to go with them because, as Cynthia whispered to Mrs Hocking, if they asked one they'd have to ask them all, at least once. They valued their privacy. In the lounge before lunch Cynthia would sometimes talk about where they planned to go.

'I know the area from my childhood,' she explained. 'So many of these lovely little places have memories for me. I always wanted to come here on holiday in the years before the war, but Frank, my husband, never cared for it. He was quite rude about it. "Just one b— peak after another," he used to say.'

'Fancy!' said Mrs Forrest. 'I can't imagine anyone disliking the Peak District.'

'I can, when I'm toiling up to the King's Head,' said Major Catchpole. 'Pixton has hills that would defeat a Sherpa.'

'To me Derbyshire beats even the Lake District,' said Miss Rumbold. 'And it's much more undiscovered.'

'Yes,' said Mrs Webber. 'Wordsworth has a lot to answer for.'

By mid-July the Webbers were accepted, admired, even loved, particularly for their devotion to each other, which all the women found 'lovely' and 'so nice to see', and which both the men kept quiet about. Their position was as part of the community at the Princes, yet somehow slightly above it. Mrs Webber reinforced this primacy by announcing that she didn't need her sweet ration because she had never had a sweet tooth, and saying that she would use it to buy sweets for general consumption – a box of chocolates if one could be found, Turkish delight or liquorice allsorts if one could not. All the residents at the Princes were enthusiastic in acclaiming her generosity, though in truth it created little pockets of animosity when one or other of them was thought to be taking more than their fair share.

It was bound to end in tears. The tabloid press understands that there is nothing the general public likes more than the building-up of a popular idol – nothing except its bringing down. The Webbers had been supplied with a pedestal. By late July it was time to blow it up from under them.

It was Mrs Phipps who provided the explosive. She

had, as everyone at the Princes knew, a weak bladder, and at some time during the night she could be relied on to get up and go to the bathroom in her corridor. As she went past the Webbers' suite one night she heard a sound and stopped. It was, she felt sure, the inner door to Mrs Webber's bedroom. She stood a second or two, waiting; then from further away she heard another door shutting – the door, it could only be, to Simon Webber's bedroom on the other side of the sitting room.

She scurried along to the bathroom, switched on the light and looked at her watch. It was half past three.

Mrs Phipps was not an ill-disposed woman, and not any more of a tittle-tattle than anyone else at the Princes. She nevertheless found it impossible to keep her information to herself. She confided the substance of it to Mrs Forrest and together they talked to Miss Rumbold, who had the reputation of being a bit of a radical, having voted Liberal several times, though of course at the last election she had voted for dear Mr Churchill. To Mrs Forrest she was a woman of standards, though when she had listened twice to the story she still felt quite troubled – her cheeks were high pink in colour, and she had to struggle to find a way through her uncertainties.

'So what you are – no, you are not implying anything – what the sounds you heard seem to suggest—'

'That's better,' said Mrs Phipps. 'I should *hate* it if—'

'Of course you would. What those sounds suggest is that the pair of them have imposed themselves on us as mother and son, whereas in fact they are . . . she is . . . *he* is . . . Oh dear. I don't know the word.'

'No,' said Mrs Forrest wistfully. 'When an older man has a younger woman for his . . . you know . . . there are quite a lot of words and phrases, some of them quite vulgar, to describe the situation.' Mrs Forrest's voice sank to a whisper. 'But this . . . Would the word "gigolo" describe him?'

'I don't know,' confessed Miss Rumbold. 'It brings to mind someone like Rudolph Valentino. Do you remember him? How my heart used to flutter! It suggests someone Latin. Someone like – would Tyrone Power fit the bill?'

'Yes, I think so,' said Mrs Phipps. 'Someone like that. I believe he's Irish. He's quite unlike Simon Webber.'

'If that is his real name. Oh, I agree. He's so tall and regular featured and fair. One would say the Aryan type if it hadn't been made a dirty word by those dreadful Nazis.'

A thought struck Mrs Forrest.

'But what about his ration book? How would he get one in the name of Simon Webber?'

'I worked in London during the war,' said Miss Rumbold darkly. 'In London you can get anything at a price. And though Mrs Webber says she only has the normal petrol ration they do get around a lot, don't they? Could they have . . . contacts?'

'What sort of contacts?'

'People with a husband in Civil Defence could still have contacts that he made in the war. Where I worked, CD officers were notorious.'

It might have seemed that a guilty verdict had already been passed, but in the end they lacked courage and decided they had to consult with someone, preferably another of the guests, so that the thing would be kept within the four walls of the Princes. Pixton was a traditional, elderly, straight-laced town, and nothing could damage the residents more than a sex scandal centred on what was now their home. In the end they decided to talk to Major Catchpole, whose first reaction was not unlike Miss Rumbold's: where she went pink he went scarlet.

'We thought,' said Mrs Phipps carefully, winding up her tale, 'that you with your greater experience—'

'Experience, dammit! I don't—' But he quietened down almost at once. It would strain belief if he denied ever having had contacts with adultery. 'But of course it's sometimes known. When I was in India there were cases of officers' wives, with subalterns, even with one of the dusky-faced johnnies, damn them. And during the war, with couples separated, and many women becoming widows . . . Stuff happens that it's better not to talk about.'

'Oh, we do agree!' said Miss Rumbold. 'We are so uncertain that we couldn't put a name to what he is.'

'What who is?'

'Simon. We finally fixed on the word "gigolo", but it doesn't seem quite right.'

'No, it doesn't. Some of the young chaps in the mess had a word for it – toyboy. But that doesn't seem quite right either. Seems a serious young man, this Simon.'

'It's the uncertainty that makes it so troubling,' said Mrs Forrest. 'There might be other explanations.'

'The question is, even if it were certain, would it be for us to judge?' asked Major Catchpole, whose military career had left him with a life's motto: anything for a quiet life.

'But if we *knew,* and did *nothing*, and it got out around the town!' said Mrs Phipps. 'The reputation of all of us would be at rock bottom! We have a certain reputation because the Princes has a certain reputation. The townspeople respect us, the spa patients and their relatives respect us. We have a position in the community out of all proportion to the rent we pay.'

Major Catchpole was quick to placate Mrs Phipps.

'Of course, of course. I'd be the last one to throw that away. But the thing is, we must be sure. We must think up a plan of campaign and when we are sure, and only then, we can decide on a strategy, think up a course of action and stick to it.'

Major Catchpole was not the only person who was decisive in theory but inconsistent in practice. That same evening he invited Mr Somervell to have a beer with him in the King's Head, and in a corner of the Saloon Bar he confided in him the gist of the two ladies' story. From that moment the battle for secrecy was lost.

When everyone in the Princes except Mrs Hocking knew what was suspected of the Webbers they became grateful for the afternoon excursions of Mrs Webber and Simon (they were no longer referred to as mother and son). That was when the rest could talk the situation over. The thing that was most difficult for most of them was the injunction that, until they were sure, no change should come over their behaviour to the pair.

'I just hate having to talk to them,' said Mrs Matthews,

a roly-poly widow with strong opinions. 'Just smiling and pretending it's all right.'

'It's the same for all of us,' said Mr Somervell.

'Oh, I know, but I just have this strong feeling, this *thing*. After all, this has always been a respectable spa town – not like Harrogate, where all sorts of things were going on. Pixton has always had genuine invalids, not people sneaking away from their families in order to have a dirty time. And an older woman, *much* older, and a very young man. My blood freezes – it really does. I can hardly stop shivering.'

The atmosphere had definitely changed, but subtly at first. The moment of transition was symbolised for Mrs Webber in the spa's conservatory – a glass attachment to the theatre, depleted by war and the terrible winter but still a gracious and heartwarming place to be as the summer sun streamed in. It was here that Cynthia Webber, strolling through on her own (Simon was at his books) and looking at plant labels and descriptions, was cut by Mrs Phipps and Mrs Forrest. She had seen them coming from the next room and prepared herself (for she was far from unobservant, and had seen how things were going) for a frosty nod or a distant 'Good morning'. In fact the two ladies, faces set firmly ahead, their steps proceeding to the tea room, ignored her entirely and did not even look away but stared straight through her. Mrs Webber did not enjoy the experience but she joked about it to herself. When that evening she told Simon he said 'Vicious old cows' and 'It's time we moved on.' She did not disagree with him.

* * *

It was two mornings after this, at breakfast, that the next change began. Mrs Hocking brought in the post when it was nearly nine and Simon had already gone on a long walk 'to think things over' he said, and was heard to say. The Webber package included a bulky, official-looking envelope which Mrs Webber opened. It was addressed to Simon, but she knew what it must be.

'Oh good,' she said brightly (she hardly ever spoke now at meals, and never initiated a conversation). 'It's Simon's passport.'

There was immediate silence, and Mrs Forrest got up. She had been feeling guilty about the brutal cutting of her fellow guest, because she was not a vicious woman.

'Oh, what a good likeness,' she said, looking at the first page of the stiff blue booklet with the royal arms on the cover.

'Yes, a friend took it, and we insisted the main thing was the likeness. Travelling in Europe is pretty problematic still, and Simon still isn't sure where he wants to go. Ah – they've got everything right: "Webber, Simon Marius, born 11th March 1928."' She looked up at her fellow lodgers. 'All absolutely correct. Simon will be pleased.'

Mrs Forrest retreated, feeling somehow ashamed. Later, when she knew Cynthia (as she now again called her) had gone out she talked the matter through with Major Catchpole and Miss Rumbold.

'It's the fact that it's a *pass*port.' she said. 'A ration book or a driving licence wouldn't be at all the same. There wouldn't be a photograph for a start, and they're easily forged or transferred. But a *pass*port. Everyone knows they don't make mistakes with those. It's as clear as clear he *is* her son.'

'They're *very* careful about passports,' agreed Miss Rumbold, 'as they have to be. All those Poles staying on after the war, and all those displaced persons coming from central Europe. The riff-raff of the world wants to come here. The authorities need to be careful, and they are.'

Miss Rumbold's radicalism, if it ever existed, did not run to showing the hand of friendship to foreigners. She even distrusted the Welsh.

'And when it comes down to it, the "evidence" was very thin,' conceded Major Catchpole, who had always exercised a restraining influence. 'The woman could have had a migraine, and the boy was getting her aspirins.'

'Oh dear,' said Mrs Forrest. 'I've been very foolish.'

'Not at all, not at all. But I think on the whole Mrs Phipps would have done better to hold her tongue. But we should have thought that older women with lovers—'

'Let's say men friends.'

'—with men friends half their age and less are not frequent, not in *this* country. I believe such . . . liaisons were common in France between the wars, and very probably are still common today. We do things differently here.'

And so opinion swung round. Mrs Forrest was crucial, since she had been the first one Mrs Phipps confided in. Everyone agreed it was a storm in a teacup. Mrs Phipps, however, was wistful about the change and said she was never going to be *quite* sure.

The change in atmosphere did not alter the decision of Mrs Webber, who had not at all liked the days of ostracism after her weeks of pre-eminence. She went to Mrs Hocking and said they would be leaving the next day, though they had paid up to the end of the week.

'I have no idea what silly story was put around,' she told the temporary manager, 'and I don't want to know. But I do know that for nearly a week we couldn't get a civil word out of anyone. I'm not used to such foolishness, and the fact that they've had second thoughts does not change my mind one little bit. I'm not used to mixing with people so feeble-minded that they alter with every change of wind. Ah – my ration book—' and indeed Mrs Hocking was handing it to her with a wistful expression, clearly wondering when next she was going to be able to let the suite. 'Please don't think I have anything to complain about with you. You may put any story about you like.'

So the next day, while Simon was stacking the suitcases in the car, the story was going round that Cynthia's father-in-law, who had never recovered from his son's death, was very poorly indeed, and they were anxious to see him one more time before . . .

On their way down towards Derby, where they had booked two single rooms, there was for a time silence in the car.

'I was not deceived for one moment by the little party waving us fond farewells,' eventually said Cynthia, knowing Simon was thinking of the same things. 'One or two of the wavers must have been the ones that started it all off.'

'Of course they did. I couldn't stand the atmosphere at the place, whether they were with us or against us.'

'They were a poor lot,' agreed Cynthia. 'Sheep led by donkeys. With hindsight we were bound to find the company unsuitable: narrow people with attitudes stuck in the Victorian age gravitate to little one-horse towns like Pixton.'

'They certainly could be vicious though,' said Simon.

'Ignorance is always vicious. And narrow. I certainly didn't go through the business of getting rid of your father to be treated by them as a scarlet woman.'

Simon laughed.

'They never even made up their minds, though – never took a line and stuck to it. One minute we were mother and son, next minute a middle-aged woman and her much younger lover.'

Cynthia put her arms around him and laughed merrily.

'Typically provincial,' she said. 'It never occurred to them that we could be both.'

Mother Dear

Our mother bore six children at a time when large families were rare, and in a small town where they were commented on with pursed lips, or accompanied by a salacious leer. I say 'my mother bore' not because we arrived from her womb (though, unlikely though that seemed to us, we did) but because our father played no part in our early lives that we can easily recall: he was always 'at work' or 'down the allotment', whence came shrivelled greens and carrots, gnarled turnips and potatoes scarred by spade marks. Our mother was our life, and I suppose that, just as a dog on a lead has his owner on a lead as well, we were hers.

She was not, I emphasise, a motherly person; nor, I imagine, did she participate joyfully in the process by which our existences were set in train. She was dour and hard, the sergeant-major of the house. I never remember her embracing me or kissing me, or any of the other five, for she had no favourites. We were her life because she organised us: as soon as we were capable of doing anything around the house we were taught it and then kept at it. Kept at it, in fact, all the hours we were home from school. Teaching these home duties was done by slaps or worse on the bare legs, or cuffs around the head. Threats kept us at our tasks, and the threats were always carried out if our efforts fell short of her expectations in any way. Our hours at school were our times of pleasure. During our hours at home we were worked as hard as any mill child or young chimney sweep in the nineteenth century.

If my mother had been a literary person one could say she had modelled herself on Mrs Joe Gargery. Hair drawn sharply back into a bun, hard features, her ruling us by her feared hand – certainly she could be said to have brought us up by hand. In fact she never read – not book nor even newspaper, which our father would often doze over. Her joy was in organising, and she spent all her spare time doing that.

Our only pleasure at home was sometimes listening to the wireless. Not while we were working: that would mean our minds were not on the menial tasks she had ordered us to do. But later just before we went to bed, she might put on the Home Service, and we might hear part of a play, the news, or a light concert. I formed my love of operetta then. It enchanted me because everybody seemed so *happy*. If my mother had not been tone deaf she would have turned it off as a bad influence.

And she would have been wise to do so. It *was* a bad influence from her point of view. It confirmed for me what I had sensed from school, that there was another way, that other families were not organised into a monstrous regiment of children, that happiness in other families, while not constant, was at least possible.

I said this to Annie, my elder sister.

'We're not like other families,' I said.

'I know.'

'They have *fun*. They have mothers who love them.'

'I know they do.'

'What should we do about it?'

'I don't know.'

That was not a very satisfactory conversation, but I remember it because it brought the subject out into the open for the first time. Of course we had had conversations – at night before bed, on the way to school – in which we said how much we hated Mother. But this one aired the possibility that something might be done about it. We considered complaining to the social services or the police, but we knew nothing about the former, not even where its offices were, and we thought we might simply be taken 'into care', which sounded vaguely threatening, like the devil you don't know. We occasionally saw a policeman or woman on the beat, but the thought of going up to him or her and complaining that our mother worked us like slaves every hour of the day, every minute we were home, was too daunting to give serious consideration to: he (or she) would probably laugh at us, and ridicule is something children hate. Or if they did see there was a problem, they would most likely call and talk it over with Mother. The consequences didn't bear thinking about.

'I don't see there's any alternative,' said Annie one day. 'We'll just have to kill her.'

I thought, then nodded, and said nothing more. The idea incubated, took on strange forms, ballooned, but the main thing was, it was there, and the next few weeks saw a great deal of discussion, vague plans.

The plan which Annie and I discussed most often was one in which all of us children had some part in the killing, so that no one of us (we thought) could be convicted of the crime of murder. For example, Mother was to be poisoned, and one child was to procure the poison, another to procure the strong drink it was to be administered in, another to put the poison in the drink, another to lure her to taste it. As a discussion topic it was admirable. We realised quite soon that we could not go into a chemist's and ask for poison over the counter, let alone one unknown to Western science (something I felt was ideal). We then talked about a break-in at the pharmacy (break-in had a nice sound involving physical action rather than a special skill) but the plan fell through when we started to talk about what it was we were trying to get hold of. We had no idea what was a poison and what was not. We might just choose a drug that would give her diarrhoea, which would be funny but wouldn't do anything to change the situation.

'We could push her over a cliff, or out of a high window,' said Annie. That would have been fine if we had not lived in a small town in Lincolnshire – county of low-lying fens. There was a distinct lack of high-rise buildings as well.

We had got no further than deciding we would say our mother had gone to help her sister in Middlesbrough, who was suffering from an inoperable (we used the word fatal, and had to explain that to the little ones) cancer, when it happened. I say, 'it happened' because that's how it felt. We had, after all the discussions, no plan, and it may have been that it was that that caused the welling up in me of a sense of frustration, of impotence, of a mother-directed rage.

It was about seven o'clock on an autumn evening. Our father had eaten his 'tea', and after a snooze had gone down to the British Legion Club, which he always did on Friday nights. He asked me to put his tools away in the garden shed, and told my little brother Martin he could put the piles of weeds that were dotted around the flower beds in the back garden on to the compost heap. Martin was – is – the best of us, the most sensible, the most brain-alive. If he had been older he would either have thought up a plan for Mother's murder or slapped down our plotting as sheer childish delusions.

It was when he was coming back from the compost heap that it happened. He had filthy hands, and not only that: he had slipped, fallen, and his short trousers were brown with leaf mould. Mother appeared at the kitchen door. Probably she had been looking through the kitchen window, awaiting disaster.

'Just look at you! Filthy child!' She grabbed from the window ledge where it always lay a little bundle of twigs with which she always beat our bare legs to relieve her feelings. 'I'll teach you to get yourself all over muck.'

She grabbed him to her. He sobbed and worked himself out of her grasp, leaving his pullover in her hands. 'You just wait, you little monkey,' she yelled, and started after him.

But she never reached him. I was collecting up Dad's

garden tools and I had just taken from off the path a heavy spade. I was a strong fourteen-year-old – made strong not by athletics or team games but by slavery around the house. I raised the spade and brought it down with all the force at my command on Mother's head. She fell forward to the ground, then rolled over, her eyes looking vengefully at me. She repeated her last words:

'You just wait, you little—'

Then she died.

I felt nothing as I looked down on her. Not grief, not guilt, not even exhilaration. Annie as usual chimed in with my reactions. She appeared at the front door and after a moment, seeing the stillness of the body, she said: 'Go and get a blanket and cover her up.'

I fetched a blanket from the top shelf of the wardrobe in our bedroom. We wrapped her in it and pulled her to a dark corner down the side of the house that had never been a home. Then we talked about what we should do when Dad came home (always, in the days and weeks ahead, we talked about our next move, never looked further into the future).

The result of this discussion was that when Dad came home we told him that we'd had a telegram from Auntie Kath in Middlesbrough, and Mother had gone by train to nurse her through cancer. Our father thought for a bit, and then said 'Oh aye?' and settled down to read the front pages of the daily newspaper.

Before he went to bed, he said: 'It's funny, your mother never had a good word to say about your Auntie Kath.'

Annie, who was proving a tower of strength, said:

'But it's cancer. That makes it different, doesn't it?'

Our father thought. 'Aye, 'appen,' he said.

That night at 2 a.m., in total silence, Annie and I buried our mother in a patch of earth at the bottom of the garden which my father had tried to turn into a vegetable patch but had given up when the soil proved too poor and too often waterlogged. With her we buried a small suitcase which our mother always kept packed with emergency things for if any of us suddenly had to go to hospital. We added two dresses of hers, a cardigan, blouse and skirt, and a great deal of unattractive underwear. The parental bedroom was at the front of the house and Dad slept on, as did the scattered neighbours. By three o'clock Annie and I were in the two undersized beds we called ours in the bedroom we shared.

Next morning Annie cooked for our dad his usual fried breakfast. 'I'll have to help with the cooking,' he said, 'while your mum's away.' He never did cook more than about once a month, but he did pull his weight by doing all the heavy shopping, the bill paying, and his usual gardening, avoiding almost all the costs of vegetables. The rest of the running of the house went like clockwork. It always had, but we did what we'd always done with much less frequency, and with a much lighter heart.

The younger children were a bit of a problem at first. We enjoined on Martin that he was to say nothing to any of them about what he'd seen. The young ones told everyone that Mummie was away, nursing Auntie, and then they forgot about her in the blessedly free and contented atmosphere that was evolving in the house.

The first problem that emerged was what to say about our mother's absence. Dad didn't mention her for days after she 'left', but as the days stretched to weeks I decided we had to make the first moves. 'I thought we'd have heard from Mum by now,' I said one night when the little ones were in bed.

'Never a great one with her pen or pencil,' said Father.

'She could telephone Mrs Cowper down the road,' I said, mentioning the only household nearby to be on the phone.

'They were never great friends,' said Dad. And that was true. Our mother had no female friends, and certainly no male ones either. It was Dad who made the next move.

'I begin to doubt your mother's coming home at all,' he said one day. ''Appen she likes being free of us.'

That was a turning point. Henceforth Mother's return was an 'if' rather than a 'when'. We heard from friends at school that down the British Legion our father had speculated about whether she'd 'found a new bloke'. We sniggered at the unlikelihood of it, but not while Dad was around. Soon we became a different family unit, one with a dad, an acting mum in Annie, and a cooperating family coping with all the duties of the household. We were a happy home. One of Dad's 'sayings', things he came out with regularly, was 'I don't think your Mum knew how to be happy.' Now we did. Her death had released us.

And we all did well. In our way we were a successful family. Martin went to university at Leeds, and later became a lecturer at Durham University. He specialised in law. Clare, the second girl, became a nurse and went out to Australia, where she married and had a family. Vince, the second boy, became a motor mechanic and was famous in the neighbourhood as one who could fathom and nurse back to health any make of motor engine. Paul, the third boy, became manager of a large bookshop. Annie – dear, 'without whom' Annie – became a primary school teacher, and had a large and wonderfully happy family.

We had reunions for many years, which sometimes even Clare managed to attend. They always made me think back to the early years of our 'liberation', when in the evenings we sat round the wireless, and eventually (a thrilling day in the family's life) the television set. We could bring friends home from school then, and Dad emerged as someone who loved having children around him. In the summer we had little treats – usually excursions: to Skegness, Cambridge and, most excitingly, to London.

I sometimes read crime novels and they never have a happy ending. Not a *really* happy one. Ours did. I shudder to think what would have become of us if we had spent all our childhood in the shadow of our mother. As it was, the liberation was quick and almost total: within a week or two laughter was heard in the house. Quite soon after that we children had spells when we were positively boisterous. That murder freed us, allowed us to be natural, allowed us to be happy.

Dad said that once, towards the end of his life. 'By 'eck, it's been a happy home, has this one,' he said. I thought he wanted to say more, get close to the reason why it had become happy, but all he followed it up with was: 'It's been happy for you, hasn't it, lad?'

'Yes, Dad,' I said. 'I've had a very happy life.'

I haven't said much about me because I was the one who stayed at home. I became an accountant, and Dad and I shared the work of the house that we couldn't get done by a cleaning lady. I knew I couldn't leave the house, not with that *thing* buried down the end of the back garden. And I couldn't bring a wife there, have children there. Anything could have happened while I was out at work, what with Dad's passion for gardening and kiddies' love for buckets and spades. It was better as it was. And there was no guarantee I could have got a wife if I'd wanted to. I was presentable enough, when I was younger, but accountancy as a job did not stir many women's blood.

Dad had a long and happy retirement. When he died of prostate cancer at the age of seventy-seven I was just fifty. He lay in the hospital bed, trying to conceal his pain, often thanking me for all I'd done for him, as he put it. One day he said:

'It turned out all right, lad, didn't it?'

'Our lives? Course they did, Dad.'

'No, I mean . . . the business with your mother.'

The nearest occupied bed in the hospital was some way away. I swallowed.

'Mother? What did you know about that?'

''Appen more than you knew. I checked on the night she disappeared that there was still the case she packed should anyone be rushed off to hospital. It was where it always was, in that old wardrobe on the landing. And I checked next day as well and it were gone. And I knew that the spade you put away in the shed had earth on it, though

I hadn't used it at all the day before. And I was bound to see where the earth had been turned over.' He took my hand, shook it, and then kissed it. 'You did a good job, David. The best thing you ever did. Don't let anyone tell you different.'

I nodded. When I thought about it, I decided the final tally concerning what I had done was not too bad: five children growing up to be fine adults, a man rescued from a hideous marriage. If I was the exception, it was because I was the one who did it. I was and am a special case. All the time I was nursing Dad I was having funny visions of bars growing inside the windows of our house, felt that the open prison I had lived in up to then was turning into a high-security one. Dad's death when it came would not release me, nor did it. I had no friends, though the family who were still around in the neighbourhood were friends, and those are the best kind.

Now I am retired, and I work in the garden, though not *there*, and listen to the radio, watch a bit of television. I like to know about other people's lives. But I like to know about them from afar: I have grown so used to my house, and sometimes it seems to me that I have always been old in it. And now I know I have come to love it. Here is enshrined everything I have achieved. I am a prisoner who has come to love his cell. Nothing is left of the David who might have been. I am watching from outside, as if I was dead. I killed our mother, and she in her turn has killed me.

The Fall of the House of Oldenborg

When he emerged from the grand audience chamber the prince was in a right pet.

'It makes me absolutely sick!' he muttered. 'Sick to the pit of my stomach. Did you hear that, Pat? The odious endearments to his new wife. My mother! The King my father not two months dead, and my mother is now my aunt and he is now my stepfather! Did you hear him calling me "son"?'

'I did, and I heard your reply, Hammy.'

A smile of satisfaction lightened his petulant face.

'Did you? Pretty neat, I thought it.'

And totally unwise, like everything he did. After a great deal of 'son' talk had made him more and more tetchy, his mother had commented on the cloudiness of his brow.

'On the contrary, I've had too much "son",' he said. Quick, I suppose, but not the way to behave in the new

King's court. Claudius is a soldier, and not to be played with.

Hammy was peeved. Naturally he was peeved. The moment his father, the old king, died, his uncle called a snap election, won it, and was crowned before Hammy could get back to the Danish capital. He was studying, as I was, at the University of Wittenburg, where he was a very ineffectual president of the Student Union. I was his deputy, and I did all the work and took all the decisions, with typical Irish efficiency. He spent most of his time in amateur dramatics – the traditional resort of the totally unserious student – which was how he acquired the diminutive of his name. I read whatever books were available in English or Latin, and financed my studies as Diplomatic and Foreign Affairs Correspondent of the *London Sunne*.

'The man is a brute!' exclaimed Hammy. 'If only I'd been here to stand against him. As it was, the Danish aristocracy was bound to elect a man of that type. They're still Vikings at heart.'

I wasn't inclined to deny, after a mere week or two of observations, that King Claudius was a thug, albeit a thug with an expensive education. Still, Hammy was deluding himself if he thought that, even if he had been on the spot, there had been any hope of his winning a disputed election. He made no decision as president of the Students' Union that he did not reverse or rescind on the morning after. Of such stuff are kings not made.

My column in the *London Sunne* was much less diplomatic and discreet than it had been under my predecessor. I was turning it into a high-class gossip column, with a strong line in royal scandals. My proprietor (an eccentric thousandaire whose place of origin is as yet undiscovered) had written to praise what he called my 'looning down' of the feature, and said he had made this a model for the work of all his other scribblers. It was for this reason, scenting scandal and blood, that I had followed Hammy to Denmark. Denmark was obviously a place where news was being made. But more than that: if Hammy had a future there, I had no objection to being his right-hand man. Nor, for that matter, if Hammy was out of the picture, to being the right hand of his uncle Claudius, though the fact that he had been heard to refer to me as an 'economic migrant' did not bode well for any future cooperation.

I had not been pleased, on my arrival, to find another Irishman already in place. His title was Deputy Armourer to the Royal Guard, but I suspected he supplemented this by spying for the English Queen's council or by scribbling for one of the *London Sunne*'s miserable competitors. I was even less pleased to see this fellow approach as Hammy spoke.

'Hello O'Ratio,' I said glumly. He gave me the most imperceptible of nods and turned at once to my companion.

'Strange news, Your Royal Highness.'

'Call me Hamlet,' said the prince. 'What news?'

'In confidence—' he drew the prince aside and continued in sibilant whispers that my newshound ears had no difficulty picking up '—the palace guards are in turmoil. They say they have seen your father.'

'My father? Impossible. They kept him on ice till I came home so I could be sure he was dead. Considerate, wasn't it?'

'His ghost. It's been seen patrolling the battlements. It was definitely seen by Barnard and Marcel.'

'Barnard!' I said scornfully. 'A credulous, dull-witted fellow, and Marcel is hardly better.'

'You weren't supposed to be listening!' O'Ratio said bitterly, turning and glaring at me.

'Well, if you will talk like a camp hairdresser who's been had by all the NCO's,' I replied . . .

That was a bit unfair. It was true O'Ratio was never to be seen in the red lantern district down by the Elsinore docks, but I had no evidence he was a pansy by nature. His friendship with Hamlet, however, was compounded of starry-eyed royalty-worship and the sort of sentimental gush that the companions of reasonably attractive young men seem to go in for. O'Ratio was a typical penniless Irish soldier of fortune, attaching himself to anyone who offered. Not surprising if he found buggery more enticing than beggary. Hammy's bedroom tastes I had had several indications of in Wittenburg.

'The ghost,' continued O'Ratio, 'has indicated a desire to talk to Your Royal Highness.'

'And by what feat of dumb crambo did the ghost convey this to a pair of dimwits like Barnard and Marcel?' I asked.

'A being from the Other Side has ways and means,' said O'Ratio.

'Quite,' said Hammy, serious. 'There are more things

in heaven and earth, Pat, than a cynical worldling like you could imagine.'

And he wandered off with O'Ratio, talking low and serious. 'I'm gonna put that white sheet on again,' I carolled, though only mentally. When I thought about it the last person I'd seen in a white sheet was Hamlet himself, playing the ghost of Julius Caesar at Wittenburg in a translation of the play by William Shaksberd (rumoured to be a pseudonym of the essayist Francis Bacon). He'd got the part because his ambitions for a crown were well-known.

I was pretty sure of what was going to happen next. Hammy was going to go up on to the battlements and the ghost would appear (in the white-sheeted person of O'Ratio or one of his soldierly mates), and take Hamlet aside and tell him he'd been murdered.

How did I know this? Because O'Ratio was one of those hangers-on of royalty who finds out what the royal personage most wants to hear, then tells him it.

I was confirmed in this view two days later when Hammy came to me all ineffectually excited and told me he'd had an encounter with the ghost of his father.

'He took me apart from the others,' he said solemnly, his language becoming suitably elevated, 'and imparted a matter of great moment.'

'Oh?' I said. 'The colour of the fourth horse of the Apocalypse?'

'My sire was murdered by his brother,' said Hammy, ignoring me. 'Claudius poured poison in his ear while he slept.'

'How does he know if he was asleep?'

'He has passed through to that state where knowledge is not limited as it is limited by our worldly state, Pat.'

'Ah,' I said. I wished he wouldn't call me Pat. Royalty should not be matey. And he should give me my title: Earl of Duntoomey, in the County of Killarney. I had no seat, no money, no post at court, but I was descended from the second last king of Ireland, on both sides of the blanket, and I wished he would use my title, to distinguish me from that direct descendent of an itinerant Irish mathematician, O'Ratio.

I was meditating how to take this matter of the supposed ghost further when we were fortunately interrupted by Ophelia, the daughter of the new king's first minister. She had been making a great nuisance of herself since Hammy's return to court. And so had her poisonous rat-pack jerk of a brother on her behalf.

'Hamlet, what ails you? What does this change towards me mean?'

'Nothing, madam, except that I have seen a wider world.'

'Before you went we had something together—'

'Nothing, madam. Nothing whatever. If you had something it was entirely in your imagination. A royal does not marry into the political class. It would destroy all our credibility.'

'But you said—'

'I said nothing. Go and find some religious order, preferably a closed one, and shut your disappointments away with others of your self-deluded kind.'

Ophelia dashed off weeping. I had little sympathy. I had every reason to doubt that Hammy had ever given cause to hope to any member of her sex. But she had given me time to think.

'Did you know there's a travelling theatre company in town?' I asked.

'Really?' said Hammy, perking up. 'Do they have any parts unfilled?'

'Nothing suitable for your rank and talents,' I said hurriedly. 'They are performing *The Mousetrap*.'

'That old thing. Everyone's seen it.'

'I doubt whether your Uncle Claudius is a great playgoer,' I said. Hammy raised his eyebrows enquiringly. 'Do you remember that bit towards the end acted in dumb show?' I asked him.

That was a cliché of that branch of the revenge tragedy commonly called the whodiddit. The audience was shown the truth of what had happened by having the murder silently re-enacted.

'The murderer comes in while – right!' said Hammy – 'while the victim is asleep.'

'Exactly. And poisons the glass of aquavit that the victim always keeps at his bedside.'

'Ah – pity . . .'

'What if you, Hammy, commanded a royal performance here at Elsinore. They're only crap actors. They'll be happy with a few ducats and a square meal. In return for all the publicity they'll get, you could persuade the manager—'

'Yes?'

'—that instead of the dumb-show murder suggested by Mr A.C., the play's perpetrator, the poison will not be put into an aquavit glass—'

'But in his ear!' Light was breaking, but slow as sun on an Irish winter morning. 'But – what then?'

'Then your eyes will be on the King. If that's how he murdered your father, his guilt will be clear to you and to the whole court.'

And if he didn't, it won't, I thought. I had no doubt that this was a story fed to Hamlet by O'Ratio and his mates, to spur Hamlet on to action, and to get themselves cushy places at court once he had gained Claudius's crown. Nice work if you can get it. Only I was determined that if anyone got it, it was going to be me.

Hamlet was in his element. He loved having actors around him, particularly bad ones. He lectured them, told them how scenes should be played, how the verse was to be spoken. They listened respectfully, and tittered behind his back, though in truth he was no worse an actor than they were.

The afternoon of the command performance came. The court assembled in the palace ballroom, where an improvised stage had been erected. The King and Queen arrived last, she with all the dignity that could be mustered by one who had married her husband's brother a month after her husband's death, he with a pretence of being a regular attender at cultural events of every kind. His steward, though, had put a bottle of aquavit (double strength Royal Danish Breweries brand, 'for added effectiveness against the grippe and the clappe') by his throne, and a large glass. He knew his man.

King Claudius just about kept awake during the play, taking copious draughts of his tipple, and even offering it jokingly to his wife, who equally jokingly slapped his hand, then sipped. At last the dumb show began. Hamlet was watching. I was watching. What I was expecting to see was nothing – business as usual. I was surprised then to observe the King shifting uneasily on his throne at the sight of the king in the play sleeping alone on a bed. Then the figure of the murderer came in. He approached the bed. He bent over the sleeping man. He took from his pocket a phial, and he brought it down towards the sleeping man's ear—

'Bloody awful play!' bellowed the King, throwing his glass at the stage. 'Ordure, pigs manure, horse droppings! I hate all poets and playwrights. Stop the rubbish. Come on, Gertrude. I'm not watching any more of this.'

Well, of course that was the end of the cultural entertainment. The court streamed out after the royal pair, Hammy came over and shook my hand in gratitude, and I noticed Ophelia in the melée slipping over and appropriating the royal bottle of state monopoly gut-rot. Me, I went off to my room in the west tower and began to pen my weekly article for the *London Sunne*. 'Danish Court in Disarray' I headed it. It began: 'Last night tensions threatened to erupt in the royal House of Oldenborg. The new Danish King attended a performance of that old chestnut *The Mousetrap*, organised by his nephew, the son of the late King who died only two months ago. When the king angrily disrupted the performance during the dumb-show, rumours began to fly around the court concerning the manner of the late King's death, which occurred while his son was studying at the prestigious University of Wittenburg. With the state machine in chaos and rumours of a possible Norwegian invasion proliferating, the international order seems threatened by a sordid family row with criminal overtones. A central figure is luscious Queen Gertrude, wife and mother of the two rival princes . . .' And so on. I signed it The Danish Bacon.

But while I was penning the sort of rubbish that my under-educated British reading public loved, my mind was active. So the King was murdered – and murdered in his sleep by having poison poured into his ear. Hammy was right. But he was right not by reason of any supposed revelation by a ghost (I am a man of the Renaissance, not some medieval superstition-monger) but because somehow O'Ratio or one of the guards had become cognisant of the secret – perhaps suspecting Prince Claudius, as he then was, and following him at night. So far I had done rather well in capitalising on O'Ratio's inept plotting. That's what I had to keep on doing. If there was going to be a new King Hamlet, the man who did the real work, as in the affairs of the Student Union of Wittenburg, was going to be me.

I went off to find him. Somewhat surprisingly I found him at the door of the royal chapel. Coming up beside him and looking through the door I saw, before the altar, King Claudius on his knees and at prayer. What did he and God have to say to one another, I wondered?

'Now might I do it, Pat,' said Hamlet.

'Well, go on and do it,' I urged. 'You'll have the support of the whole court, after his exhibition of guilt today.'

But of course Hammy was not displaying a resolution for action, merely putting the point of view that he would immediately contradict.

'What, and send his soul straight to heaven?' he demanded. 'As the souls of those killed in prayer immediately do go?'

'Your theology is positively Dark Ages,' I said. 'Nobody in their senses believes that sort of stuff now.'

'I couldn't take the risk,' said Hammy.

'Then what are you going to do? Raise an army and start a civil war? With you two at each other's throats in the country, and Fortinbras coming from the north with a force of fresh Norwegian troops, you'd be handing him the country on a plate.'

'Hmmm,' said Hammy. 'This needs thinking about.'

'Quickly,' I urged.

But by now things were moving at double time at Elsinore. We had no sooner got back to the main body of the castle, where the Queen was distractedly looking for a bottle of something to calm her frazzled nerves, than the court was electrified by the appearance of the Lord Chamberlain at the great door in obvious perturbation.

'Your Majesty, Ophelia is dead.'

'Dead? But how!'

'Drowned, my lady.'

'Drowned?' She threw a look of reproach at her son. 'Disappointed in love, poor girl. Betrayed by one she believed she could trust. No doubt she walked into the river, letting her court dress hold her up until the weight of the water pulled her down to the reeds below.'

'Not quite, Your Majesty. She slipped on a muddy patch on the river bank and died with her head in the water clutching a bottle of aquavit.'

'I knew it was somewh—' began the Queen, but there came a second interruption. I think I've mentioned Laertes – a loud-mouthed and poisonous nerd whose idea it had been to hitch his sister up with Hammy. If this alliance (of whatever sort) had come about, his low-born family's grip on the levers of power would have been unbreakable. Now that ambition was shattered, and he burst into the great chamber making an almighty fuss and noise. He was followed by his father Polonius, looking as if his politician's instinct to be all things to all men was affecting his mental grasp. Laertes, as usual, had to hold the floor.

'Where is he? Where is that trifler with a young girl's affections? Where is that so-called *prince*? Where is he?'

'Here,' said Hammy, coming forward with chin raised, with an expression of disdain perfected for Julius Caesar being petitioned at the Capitol.

'What have you to say to my poor sister's death – you who drove her to it?'

'I no more drove her to it than I drove her to drink. It was your preposterous ambitions drove her to get ideas above her place. A prince marries a princess.'

'As, I suppose, a king marries a queen,' sneered Laertes, looking towards Gertrude. 'If there is one *available*.'

Hamlet started towards him (Hammy let no one insult his mother but himself), but to keep the initiative Laertes removed his glove and whipped it across Hammy's face.

'I challenge you to a duel,' said Hammy.

'I've already done that,' said Laertes. 'That's what the glove means.'

'Enough!' shouted the King, entering from his prayers. 'A duel there shall be.'

You can say what you like about the old King – courtiers were muttering as they discussed this development behind their hands in nooks and corridors (and what they mostly said about him was that he was much too fond of aquavit, and he turned, if not a blind, then a bleary eye to his wife's serial infidelities) – but he would never have allowed an upstart politician's brat to challenge a royal prince. Laertes would have been shipped off down to the Danish equivalent of the Tower of London with a price on his head (fifty kroner for a nice clean cut). The fact that this did not happen said something about Claudius's indebtedness to the Amundsen family, father and son.

Before the day was out many had made their way to the back door of the health food shop near the vegetable market, the standard source for effective and out-of-the-way poisons in Elsinore. The whole thing seemed to be getting out of my hands, and I was reduced to trying to ensure that Hammy remained alive.

'How can you be sure that Laertes won't be fighting with a poisoned sword?' I asked him.

'I shall reject the swords supplied by the king and insist that he choose a sword from one of the royal guards,' he said. 'There are ten guards on duty, and he can choose at random.'

'He will insist that you choose yours from one of the guards as well.'

'Very well, it will be a fair fight.'

'Laertes was champion fencer at the Copenhagen

University Fencing Club,' I said meaningfully.

'A provincial establishment, our university,' he said airily, 'fit only for the boors and bumpkins who attend it.'

'Academically laughable,' I agreed. 'The university is notable only for its jousting, its beer drinking and its swordsmanship. Laertes was the best from among the best in the world.'

Hammy thought.

'Then I shall make sure all the guards' swords are smeared with poison. Then a mere scratch will kill him.'

'His sword will be poisoned too. A mere scratch will kill you too.'

'Hmmm . . . Advise me, for God's sake, Pat! That's what you're here for!' The note of panic in his voice boded ill.

I told him I had a plan, and when darkness came I slipped off to Mensana, the health food shop. I went to the back door, but there stood a hard-faced lad handing out queue tickets with times scrawled on them. I filled in the hour and a half between with a visit to the red lantern district and a girl from Belfast who was earning her ticket home and reduced her prices to anyone with an accent that made her nostalgic.

When I returned to Mensana I was shown into a dark back room in which sat a figure of indeterminate sex with whom I was forced to communicate in dog Latin.

'This concerns a duel, I would guess,' said its hoarse voice.

'Yes. We fear poisoned sword-tips,' I said.

'Client confidentiality forbids—' it began.

'Of course, of course. But I wondered if there was

something that could be administered *before*—'

'To kill?'

'No. Preferably something to disable for combat – something that will prevent the victim from performing at the top of his bent.' There was a few seconds' silence.

'Balance . . . Successful swordsmanship depends on balance. Administer this and the . . . the patient will have the gait of a newborn calf for twenty-four hours thereafter.'

'And how is it administered?'

'For maximum effect, in the ear while sleeping.'

I laughed out loud at that. Perfect! There were problems, of course, but I thought that with O'Ratio one of the big cheeses in the Royal Guard I could surely get one of the men who guarded Laertes while he slept – and someone would, Claudius would see to that – to do the necessary for a bag of kroner. Hammy was in fact my main problem.

'From now on,' I told him, 'we are inseparable. I send out for food to town. You drink nothing but wine from my own store.'

'But I don't like your wine. You have rotten, English taste. I prefer my own wines.'

'They could be already poisoned. In Claudius's court you are worth killing, while I am not. When it comes to the fight I shall hold goblets of both wine and water, and you will drink nothing else. There will be bottles of wine and jugs of water set out for the contestants. Don't touch them.'

'You'll have to remind me.'

'Oh, for heaven's sake!' I said disgustedly. 'Whose life is this I'm protecting?'

Anyway, that showed me there could not be a moment's relaxation in my vigilance. We had a disgusting pork chop meal sent up from the Kongelig Dansk Hotel in town, and then I locked the bedroom door and we settled down to get what sleep we could. Heaven knows what rumours started going round the court. My only concern was whether O'Ratio would manage to get the destabiliser administered into Laertes's ear. One thing was in our favour: it would be just like Laertes to sleep soundly, so hideously confident as he always was.

The great hall next day was stripped for action. All furniture had been moved to the walls, and the great central area was bare. Claudius was no doubt used to masterminding such affairs of honour from his army days. At the far end of the hall were two thrones, and on the table in front of them bottles, a carafe and goblets. The King and Queen were already seated when Hamlet and I arrived. When the King saw I was carrying a bottle and a glass a shadow passed over his face. Hammy cast a glance at the two épées laid out at either end of the long table.

'Your Majesty, I demand fresh swords.'

'Fresh swords?' All injured innocence.

'Swords I can trust. I demand that we choose swords from those borne by the royal guards.'

He gestured in the direction of the assembled picked troop. The king hummed and hahed. Then he gave way. He knew the abilities as swordsmen of his stepson and his first minister's son, and he trusted to the latter's superiority.

'Very well. When Laertes arrives – ah, here he is.'

But the words almost died in his throat. Weaving his way like a drunken porter Laertes came into the hall, lurching from left to right, stumbling, and finally weaving his way erratically up to the thrones.

'Your Majesty, I demand a postponement! I have been poisoned! You see the result. Please God it does not prove fatal.'

'Hah!' said Hamlet, with an expression of stage disgust. 'The man's feigning. He's an arrant coward. The court yesterday saw whose the offence was – a rank insult to the blood royal. I demand satisfaction now, at the place and time Your Majesty appointed.'

Now the King really was in a quandary. He knew that his behaviour at the play the day before had sent waves of suspicion rippling through the court. To be seen to favour his first minister's son – the upstart grandson of Jens Amundsen, a backstreet fishmonger – over his stepson would set tongues wagging furiously. At this point O'Ratio made a rare positive contribution.

'Your Majesty, I pray this unhappy matter be settled with all speed. The Norwegian threat is imminent. There are rumours of a landing—'

'Very well. The contest will take place,' the King said, with palpable reluctance. An expression of arrant terror suffused Laertes's face. Everyone in the room must have suspected that he had been set on to challenge Hamlet by the very man who now signed his death warrant.

The swords were chosen, directions given. Laertes made desperate attempts to gain some kind of control of his movements.

'Swords at the ready!' said the King, his voice quivering. 'Let battle commence.'

Laertes lurched forward, his sword flailing. Hamlet parried it a couple of times, then he stood back, sword raised. His adversary saw his next move, and a look of pleading came into his eyes. Hamlet plunged his sword through his heart.

Advantage Hamlet.

He pulled out the sword, dripping blood on to the flagstoned floor, then he turned and bowed to the two thrones. He went forward.

'Oh, the poor young man,' said Queen Gertrude. 'And his poor father. To have lost both his children! Hamlet, are you all right?' Her priorities seemed less than motherly. Confused, she bent forward and picked up a goblet full of red wine from the table.

'Gertrude!' said the King.

'I am faint. Hamlet, you are sweaty and scant of breath. Drink too.'

'Hamlet!' I shouted, running from the far end of the hall. As I reached the table he was quaffing deep. As he set down the goblet he caught sight of his mother: her face was blue and she was struggling for breath. His eye went from her to the King, guilt deeply etched on his sensual, cunning face.

'Murderer. Twice, thrice murderer! Die thyself!'

And he plunged his sword into the guilty King. At last the blood of the Kloakkgate fishmongers was mingled with that of the Oldenborgs. Hamlet sank to the floor. I knelt down beside him and began to press his stomach, trying to make him vomit up the deadly draught. He too was going blue, he too breathing with difficulty. All my efforts were in vain, but as I pressed and struggled I heard a commotion at the great hall door. I turned and looked. Coming under the great arch, flanked by a fearsome troop of men, was a superb armoured figure, six feet or more in height, proportionately broad, fair of beard and hair, steely of eye. He advanced at the head of his army. Fortinbras!

He came towards us, his cold eye observing the scene. His demeanour seemed to say that he'd seen worse sights on the field of battle, but not many. He stopped beside Hamlet, looking down on him from his great height. The prince half-opened his eyes and spoke his dying word.

'Dishy!'

The breath left his body. The face of the invading prince was twisted with disgust.

'How absolutely vile! I had heard the Danish court was a sink of iniquity, but this is beyond anything. The realm needs cleansing – needs a purging of the rottenness and foulness which has infected it to the heart. I shall use the gallows and the stake should they be necessary, but I shall bring back decency and godliness to this unhappy land. It will be my first priority as king.'

My heart sank. I knew those tones, those absolutes. I'd heard them in my native land. Thus spoke the upright Ulsterman with a mission, and a sword to enforce it. Thus speak men who know that God is on their side, and all decent men too. It was the authentic voice of the Moral Majority.

Flee it, I thought.

Gone were all hopes of serving this or that Danish

king. I had thought to bring international sophistication to the Danes' conduct of foreign affairs, but serving in an administration formed by King Fortinbras would be a nightmare. As soon as it was safe to do so I stuffed my belongings into a backpack and scuttled down to the docks. As luck would have it I found a fishing vessel ready to depart for Aberdeen. I breathed a sigh of relief as we crossed the bar and headed for the North Sea.

Thinking it over, the idea of Scotland appealed to me. The cussed old English Queen had, as near as dammit, named the King as her preferred successor. A fine, learned man, James VI, or so I'd heard. He had his drawbacks: a Danish queen and an anti-smoking obsession. But on the plus side he had two fine sons, a ready wit, and strong views on the divine rights of kings. He would need advice from some worldly-wise figure, someone with connections to the courts of Europe. Yes, there was no doubt about it: the Stuarts were the coming men. With my help they could become the foremost dynasty in Europe. I made a firm resolve to hitch my waggon to the rising star of the Stuarts!

Where Mongrels Fear to Tread

Svein slowed down the car as we approached Fredshavn, probably to think. Svein can't drive fast and think at the same time, and he'd said to me as we set out: 'Everything has got to be done *just right,* Loyd.' That was no doubt why he'd put me straight on the back seat. He doesn't mind me in the front seat if he forgets, but at other times he says it looks cutesy and odd, a dog on the front passenger seat. I can see through that sort of flannel. He's afraid people will think he's my chauffeur (which is pretty much what he is). But today, as we approached the high wrought-iron gates, I sat there unprotesting, so that everything was *just right.*

Wrought-iron gates! you might think. I certainly did. Hardly a Norwegian touch. And that was only the start. Svein had to pull up in front of them, then get out and ring the bell on the right gatepost. Soon he was talking into thin air, then he jumped back into the car as the gates began swinging open to allow our admittance into the estate called Fredshavn. As we moved forward towards the distant white house they closed silently behind us. We could be in Martha's Vineyard or Zurich. 'Great wealth walks silently,' said the social philosopher dog Heidegger (fl. Trondheim 1920s). But he might have added that silently-walking money feels horribly creepy to those of us in the real world.

The hedges surrounding the estate, and the little box ones in the garden, were trimmed to within an inch of their lives, apparently with nail scissors. The grass was the same. No leaf, no blade was allowed the liberty of sprouting further than its fellows. All sign of individuality or enterprise was suppressed: all marched along like a splendidly-honed crack regiment, one body, not a thousand men. It was all very depressing.

'We're mixing above our station,' said Svein. 'No leaving your calling-card here, old boy.'

And the truth was, I wouldn't have dared.

We pulled up on a circular drive situated outside the front door. The door itself immediately opened, and a small man in something rather like a waiter's gear slipped out.

'If you could put your car over by the stables?' he suggested insinuatingly, as if we had very nearly committed a serious *faux pas*. Svein nodded, drove over, then walked back to the house.

'Keep it in, Loyd,' he whispered.

'If you'd come this way, Herr . . . er . . .' said the small man, whose accent was south Norwegian, but whose inbuilt (or feigned) servility was all his own. In the hall he hesitated. 'The dog . . .?'

'Comes with me,' said Svein, to his credit. 'He's part of the package.'

'Aaah . . . Well, if you'll come with me? . . . The family is still at *middag*. I'm sure they won't be long.'

Our time had been specified, five forty-five, and we had arrived on the dot. The thought occurred to both of us that we had been intended to arrive during the family's *middag* to be kept waiting until they had finished it. We did not expect any explanation to be offered.

'I used to know police chiefs like this,' whispered Svein to me as we waited in a little anteroom. 'They'd give you an appointment for ten minutes before there was any chance of seeing you. Make sure you were sweating before the session even started.'

It was in fact twenty minutes before the manservant came back and invited us into the dining room to take coffee with the family. He once more gave me an old-fashioned look, but I was beginning to get the idea that he was finding the situation rather humorous. When we got into the large, light, airy room Svein pointed to a position by the door, from which I could take in the whole situation.

We were definitely mixing with our betters. The dining table was long and elegant, though only three people were eating at it. The three places had had removed all but the wine glasses and coffee cups, but those things and the central vase sparkled, sat elegantly, told the spectator how recherché and expensive everything was. Seated there, dressed formally, was a man in his early forties, a woman probably answering to mid-thirties, and a girl of about twelve.

'Ah, Herr . . . er . . . urm. Will you take coffee?'

He made it very clear that inviting Svein to partake of

anything with the family, even so usual a thing as a cup of coffee, involved stooping. He introduced himself, his wife and his daughter, and they all sat down.

So here we were, among the nearest thing the Norwegian nation has to an aristocracy: Hans-Egil Fjørtoft, ship-owner, his wife Anne-Marie, and his daughter Ingrid. All three made a gesture towards making us welcome by quick, tight smiles. The daughter probably knew no better, poor thing. She would never have known anything else.

When Svein had been helped to coffee and had taken his suicidal amount of sugar in it, Herr Fjørtoft cleared his throat and began a clearly well-prepared introductory speech.

'You'll be wondering why I called you. It is not without a great deal of thought that I've done so, but the truth is I need help of your particular kind.' (He made it sound like drain clearance.) 'You may not know that I – and before me my father – have built up a collection of Norwegian art over the years—' He broke off to wave a hand in the direction of a picture on the wall.

'Harriet Backer,' said Svein.

Herr Fjørtoft was clearly impressed. He didn't know Svein had seen it on the cover of a 'Classics of the Hardangerfiddle' CD.

'That's my latest acquisition, bought last month. But, on my father's initiative, we've specialised in Munch. In particular we have a very rich collection of the many variations he made of his most famous picture.'

No doubt thinking to be amusing, Svein, who one can't

take anywhere, opened his mouth, spread out his hands, and let out a peculiar noise. I gained the idea that the picture was called *The Howl.*

'Very comical,' said Fjørtoft, tight-lipped. 'Yes, that picture. The number of preliminary studies and later variations on the components of that picture go into three figures.' (The man obviously thought in the number of figures any deal involved – pathetic.) 'We have forty-seven studies. We regard our collection as something held in trust for the Norwegian people.'

Oh yes? I thought. And how many sweaty, jeans-clad, haversack-carrying ordinary Norwegians have been asked into the house to view the collection that you are holding in trust for them? 'When someone says they're doing something for your benefit,' said the revolutionary dog thinker Che (fl. Hammerfest 1960s), 'go and curl up in a corner and get out your reproachful expression.'

Before Svein had finished the syrupy coffee he so enjoyed, Herr Fjørtoft stood up.

'Perhaps we should go and see the collection,' he said, in his lemon-sorbet sort of voice. We all began trooping out into the hall, but Frau Fjørtoft said off-handedly 'I think I'll give this a miss,' and started up the stairs. Her husband did not react, and unlocked a door in a far corner of the hallway. We went into a small but light room, whose walls were full of engravings, lithographs, ink drawings and smallish colour pictures. All were versions of a weird-looking woman in a night landscape, her mouth open in a howl.

'As you will see,' he said in his passionless voice, 'there are watercolour versions, lithographs, and so on, all variations either of the central woman of the picture, or of other elements in it. And we are always on the look-out for others,' he went on, still curiously uninterested in his manner of talking. 'There are still many such images in private hands.'

'Isn't it exciting?' said Ingrid, in her breathless, schoolgirl way. 'Daddy says it's one of the dominating images of the twentieth century.'

'And one day it will be yours,' he said without emotion.

So much for it being in trust for the Norwegian people. Since he could hardly be much more than in his early forties, that left him with thirty or forty years in control of the collection, with a like number for Ingrid later. Svein nodded, not commenting. And then he said:

'Are there any of these of especial value?'

'No. All are *quite* valuable, but their real worth is as a collection. Of course we let Munch scholars see them, if suitable arrangements can be made and watertight references are given.'

'I see. Now I think I should meet your staff, and see also the reason you have become uneasy.'

Fjørtoft nodded, and led the way back to the hall. Here, though, he held back and let Ingrid take the lead, ushering us into a large kitchen, relic of the early twentieth-century lavishness favoured by Norwegian ship-owners who did well out of the Great War that their homeland did not participate in. The staff were seated round the table, eating their meal after preparing and serving the family meal. There were seven of them.

'I suppose you met Mats,' said Ingrid, girlish still, but trying to be grown up. 'He's our butler, or major-domo, or general head man. And this is Chris Farraday, my governess and companion.' She had indicated a young woman in her twenties – dark-haired, self-contained and intelligent. 'She eats here because she's trying to learn Norwegian.' When Svein looked surprised, she added: 'We don't talk much at dinner . . . We're not good talkers at all . . . And this is Vidar, our gardener, who has help from the village.' Of course Vidar was in his forties, silent, capable-looking, and he nodded acknowledgement. 'This is Wenche, our cook.' The same age, stout, quiet, but with an incipiently satirical expression. 'And there are Siri, Bente and Gry, who are sort of maids – they'd normally be gone by this time, but Daddy asked them to stay since you were coming.'

Svein nodded. 'He was right. Because I need to make clear to you that what seems to be going on here is the work of a gang of art thieves – local, national, international.' He was becoming expansive, but to my ears his tone was gaining that unconvincing edge that told me he was telling porkies, or something a lot less than the whole truth. He had been told something by Hans-Egil when he was first called in that suggested to him an inside job. 'So you're not under suspicion or observation, but what I need from you is that you go about your everyday tasks, your comings and goings, in the way you've always gone about them. What *you* do may influence when the thieves decide to strike.' He turned to the maids. 'So today is an exception. In future you come and go in the regular way, understood?'

They nodded the glum assent of wage slaves who can't

wait to get away to Bergen, Hamburg or Soho. We went back to the hall where Fjørtoft was waiting for us uneasily. I guessed he never went into the servants' quarters. He led the way through the front door and round the house to the windows of the Munch room. He said, tight-lipped:

'I mentioned on the phone the two pictures which had been misplaced.' He spoke with contained fury, like a Spanish Inquisitor speaking of an arcane blasphemy. 'Then there was *this*.'

Svein examined the wood around the area where, inside, there was a latch. There were a series of random knife-cuts.

'Ah yes. There seems to have been an attempt at a break-in,' he said, his voice now unmistakably his lying one. What we had there was not an attempt at a break-in but an attempt to suggest a break-in. 'They would of course have set off the security alarms if they had succeeded.'

'Of course,' said Fjørtoft. 'One can only enter the room through the door from the hall that we used earlier, and then one must turn off the security switch just inside the door within two seconds of entering.'

'How many keys are there to that door?'

'One, mine. Oh, and one in my strongbox at Bergens Privatbank. In case of an accident, or something happening when I am abroad.'

'That seems satisfactory. And now, if you will allow us, Loyd and I will walk around the grounds to see all possible means of access to the property.'

'Is that necessary? Fredshavn is extremely secure.'

'So was the National Gallery in Oslo,' said Svein. Fjørtoft looked taken aback, but he departed bad-temperedly.

'Ha! Got him there, didn't I, old boy? That was where the oil painting of *The Scream* was stolen from in the 1990s.'

So it was *The Scream*, was it? I preferred my version. More canine, more desperate. As we walked around, Svein talked, as usual.

'Cold old house, isn't it? Cold old household too. It's like going for a stroll in the Antarctic. You hear the ice floes crack and the icebergs collide. Not much fun growing up in a place like that. Or being the wife either, come to that. It's like Frau Fjørtoft had had a general anaesthetic or two, and not completely come out of them. Funny lot. Not really of this world. They think we accept that it's an outside job, but we don't, do we, old boy? Of course the obvious one to suspect is Hans-Egil himself. Staging a robbery to collect the insurance. Nobody goes by ship these days, do they, apart from cruises. Maybe the firm is on the rocks . . . Hello, what's that?'

I had seen him already and nudged Svein's ankles. It was a young man, maybe twenty, who was cutting away ruthlessly at a young tree. Svein turned on his heels and walked back to the house. He poked his head through the windows of the large kitchen and beckoned to Mats the butler.

'Who's that boy I saw working over towards the east corner?'

Mats scratched his head.

'Boy? Oh, that will be Semyon. One of these asylum people. Come from Chechnya or some such place. Works in one of the Bergen parks, and as a part-timer with us. Sleeps in the old stables.'

'Why didn't you mention him?'

'Didn't cross my mind, to tell you the truth. He can't speak Norwegian or English, so he doesn't communicate with any of us. Just comes and collects whatever's going to eat, and takes it back to the stables.'

'Right . . . Well, we're off to find out what we can about recent art thefts.'

Svein raised his hand and turned towards the car.

'Poor young Semyon,' he muttered. 'Oliver Twistsky. And even Oliver had a few mates to talk to.'

We'd seen the TV version. I thought Bill Sykes's dog was a bit of a prat. Fancy throwing yourself off a roof for a man! We got into the car and drove to the gates, which opened for us. Svein drove about a quarter of a mile on the road towards Bergen, then drove the car into the shelter of a coppice and we trudged back towards the gates of Fredshavn, and a collection of hillocks and minor plateaus on the other side of the road. Svein selected one nicely shielded with trees, and we settled down with a pair of binoculars and kept our attention fixed on the distant white wooden house – not cosy and welcoming, as most of them are, but cold and antiseptic.

'One room lit up at one end of the first floor, another room lit up at the other end of the same floor. Bedrooms? I rather fancy they could be suites – plenty of space for *two* rooms each side . . . Ah, there's Hans-Egil, if he'll allow the familiarity . . . Damn. Can't see him, but I'd be willing to bet I know what he's doing . . . Yes, see how he's holding his arm. Crooked with the hand a bit below nipple level . . . Yes, that's definitely a glass he's holding. And it is now precisely seven forty-five.'

Svein was enjoying himself. Ten minutes later the fragrant but near-silent Anne-Marie was similarly to be seen at the other end of the first floor, fetching herself liquid refreshment. We watched for two hours, and she renewed her glass three times, her husband four. We both left for home, well satisfied with our night's work.

Over the next few days we reported back regularly to Fredshavn. We seldom saw Anne-Marie Fjørtoft, but if the master of the house was about his shipping business we left messages (but not about things of any importance) with Mats, Ingrid or the governess. Around Bergen we made enquiries, Svein using his old police connections, about art thieves, the fallout from the Oslo Munch theft, and, very discreetly, about the Fjørtoft fortune, which, disappointingly, seemed to be doing very nicely thanks all the same. From time to time we saw Semyon, the asylum seeker from Chechnya, working in one or other of the parks.

'Time to keep an eye on him,' said Svein, when a fortnight had gone by and we felt things were returning to normal at Fredshavn, after the disruption of our appearance there.

Keeping an eye on him was very easy. He did his work, talked to no one except his supervisor, ate from a packet presumably prepared at Fredshavn, and, after four-thirty, caught the bus back there. We were disappointed, and bored, after the first two days of watching him. The third day, Wednesday, however, was obviously his half day. After work he walked to a photocopying shop in Kong Oscarsgate, went in, and stayed there for over an hour. He was carrying a small bag, such as he had with him every day, and when he came out we couldn't detect by his walk that it was significantly lighter or heavier. He went to the bus station and caught an early-afternoon bus back to Fredshavn.

'It's odd, the whole situation,' said Svein. 'I wouldn't have thought the Fjørtofts were the sort of charitable people with a soft spot for asylum seekers. Cheap labour is why they employ him, I would have thought. Always unwise for rich people to do that.'

Every day, at different times, we made sure we were seen around Fredshavn, but not too conspicuously. We went to the Munch room, with Hans-Egil's key, inspected the security, noticed no change in the prized contents. I still thought she was howling ('Bitches howl before you've even got a good bite in' – the masculinist dog Hemingway, Stavanger 1960s). We swapped words with all the servants, indoor and out, with Ingrid and her governess-companion. That last, with the discretion of her kind, told us the Fjørtofts had been 'very kind' to her. We didn't seek interviews with the ridiculously buttoned-up Hans-Egil, but we left him a report every couple of days. Anne-Marie seldom appeared. Either she was participating in a social round, or she was 'indisposed'. In bed with a bottle that meant, most likely. I must admit I don't really *get* alcohol. Svein says it has the same effect as catnip on felines, but I never notice them totally insensible and gone to the world for hours at a time. More's the pity!

Svein was just forming an action plan, which would probably have failed dismally, when we were suddenly handed a missing piece in the jigsaw – though Svein, inevitably, was too slow on the uptake to take advantage of it. We were driving through Lille Lundegårdsvann, slowly following Semyon on his way to the bus station, when emerging from the art gallery called the Rasmus I saw Meyer Samling, a leggy blonde with hair stretching down to her shoulders in gorgeous profusion, wearing a sleeveless, above-the-knee frock that showed off her fashionable slimline figure. I blinked . . . I knew . . . surely I knew . . . I blinked again.

I was in the back seat at the time. I put out my right paw and scratched, scratched, scratched Svein's back.

'What's up, boy? Not feeding time yet.'

Of course it's not bloody feeding time yet! I went to extreme measures, brought both paws into play and bang bang banged them both into his back and gazed intently through the window.

'What is it, Loyd? Yes, she is a smasher.' (Svein's slang is very dated). 'Bit out of my league. You know I'm past all that.'

Oh, I knew it. And so did his ex-wife, and her bus-driver lover. I gazed through the window, whined, and let out a tremendous howl.

'Yes, you like her too.' She was now only a few yards away from the car. 'Wait a minute . . . That face rings a bell . . . But it can't be!' I barked applause. 'That's Ingrid Fjørtoft!'

She turned off into a one-way street, and it wasn't our one way. We drove round in a square to pick up her traces, and coasted round the area for over twenty minutes. Well done, Svein! You really are quick on the uptake!

So we'd established that things in the Fjørtoft household were not quite what they seemed. I did rather fear that Svein was going to misunderstand seriously the matter of young Ingrid, but I had to admit that he made a sensible decision: to clear up the subsidiary matter of the monkey before going seriously all-out to catch the organ grinder. He rang the central office of the Fjørtoft shipping line, asked for a meeting with Hans-Egil the next day, and was told that he was always in Oslo throughout Wednesday, sometimes into Thursday morning. So Semyon's half-day coincided with Fjørtoft's day in the Oslo office, freezing the computers into meltdown and the firm's secretaries into chastity. Maybe a coincidence, but maybe organised by Semyon in whatever language (sign, perhaps) he used to communicate to his bosses in Bergen.

The next day was Wednesday, and it was a doddle. Everything went as in the previous week, except that after Semyon, again clutching a small bag, had been in the premises in Kong Oscarsgate for ten minutes, Svein and I followed him. He was not in the outer office, but Svein marched straight through to the inner one (Bergen people are not used to crime or its detection, so he did it with only a minor squawk of protest from the girl on the desk), and there all the elements were: Semyon, a drably-dressed Russian-speaking operative, a large but impressively businesslike machine, and – still in its frame – an ink and colour version of several of the faces from Munch's pictures: top-hatted men and bonnetted women from his picture of Karl Johansgate, within the swirling landscape of *The Scream*.

Semyon immediately and at enormous speed started explaining in Russian, Chechnyan or something. The operative held up her hand to him and immediately turned to us and started to explain in prim, textbook English.

'I will explain. What you are seeing here is the most up-to-date process of reproduction, developed in Moscow, which can make a copy of a picture or a document which is undistinguishable, except to experts, from the original. I will not explicate further for reasons of commercial confidentialness. In Russia, misfortunately, is much thievery from museums and galleries, and today we are using very much this process to provide visitors with perfect copies to keep safe the precious originals.'

'I see,' said Svein. 'But this picture—'

'Does not come from a museum, no. We are expanding our operation into Europe and America to provide service to museums and private collectors. I receive phone call from Mr – is difficult.'

'Fjørtoft?' suggested Svein.

'Exactly. It was from this Mr Something's secretary. He want our perfect copies of his entire collection of Munch lithographs, watercolours, oils and cetera. One will be brought each week until the collection of copies is complete. I ask for signed authorisation and some payment in advance, and she send it. This one is the seventh I undertake.'

'The seventh. I see. And the secretary's name?'

'Is Miss Olsen.'

'I see. A common name. However not the name of anyone in Hr Fjørtoft's employment.'

She looked, or perhaps pretended to look, surprised. She

offered no resistance when Svein, having pointed out that she'd been duped and should have checked the authorisation and signature, removed Semyon and his framed Munch to the car. He phoned the University Russian Department, asking them if they could provide a student interpreter. We picked him up in the car, and then began the drive out to Fredshavn.

I have to say that Svein was doing rather well so far. The boy was learning, obviously from working all the time with me. With time he could make a perfectly competent assistant. However his conversation in the car – not greatly helped by the Bolshie interpreter, who was obviously convinced that Svein was setting the boy up in order to get him expelled from the country – got nowhere very interesting. It was only when we arrived at Fredshavn and went through the ridiculous business with the gates that he really got to the nub of the matter.

'So this was simply a matter of getting paid to do the job,' he asked him. 'Who paid you?'

'The teacher,' said the interpreter after consultation.

'And did she act as the go-between with the pictures?'

Again there was an incomprehensible discussion.

'No – it was the younger one.'

'Ah, the young one,' said Svein.

'The younger one.'

We were coasting through the nail-scissored lawns towards the facade of the house when I saw some way away, under a cherry tree I itched to water, Anne-Marie. She was talking to Vidar the main gardener. Body language did not suggest they were talking about topsoil or slug control. Good for her, I thought. She's found a way out of the icebox.

We were met again by Mats the major-domo at the front door, and Svein asked if the whole household could be assembled in the dining room.

'You mean the servants?' Mats asked, frowning. 'I'm not sure that Herr Fjørtoft—'

'I mean the whole house, family and servants. I believe Herr Fjørtoft is in Oslo, so what he doesn't know—'

Mats looked as if what he didn't know usually didn't remain unknown for long, but he nodded. I was rather surprised when he went out on to the steps and with a gesture summoned Anne-Marie and Vidar to the house. No prizes for guessing who was the freezer of the household, and why everyone was so much more relaxed when he was not there. Svein dallied for a moment, let Anne-Marie pass into the house first – quite the gentleman – and then he went in himself with the gardener. We and he both qualified as 'outside help', I suppose.

They all sat around the table, looking at us. Svein fetched a couple of chairs and set them by the door for Semyon and his interpreter. We stood there for a moment by the door, looking at the household: all female, apart from Mats and Vidar. Chris Farraday the governess was smiling a secretive, confident smile. Ingrid was less sure of herself, on the surface, but she gave encouraging smiles to Chris. I flopped down on the floor with a truly canine sense of drama. Now, after I've done all the hard work, I seemed to be saying, it's all up to Svein.

'I've brought you all here today,' said Svein, 'because

there's been an important development in the matter of the Munch pictures, and I think you all ought to hear about it. I have discovered that your assistant gardener from Chechnya' – he gestured towards the door – 'has been taking pictures from the Munch room in to Bergen, to a firm which offers an unusual service: a new and revolutionary process developed in Russia to provide near-perfect copies of pictures and documents – copies that only prolonged and intensive inspection can distinguish from the real thing.' There was a buzz of conversation, and much looking at Semyon. Only Anne-Marie looked bored: the body language said that she'd had it up to *here* with Munch. 'I may say that I have no evidence of Semyon – I won't attempt the surname – of Semyon's involvement other than as carrier. He was paid a small sum to take the pictures backwards and forwards. Paid by Miss Farraday here.'

'So he says,' said Chris Farraday, apparently unperturbed.

'Exactly. But I think it would be much easier for you, Miss Farraday, to gain admittance to the collection. I have not heard of Semyon going anywhere in the house other than the kitchen. Mostly he's kept out in the stables.'

'We used to say the attics were for mice and the north Norwegians,' said Anne-Marie, suddenly waking up. 'Dear Hans-Egil goes one step further for asylum seekers.'

'Ah!' said Svein, quite eloquently. 'Now Semyon also says that the pictures to be copied were conveyed to him by young Ingrid here. If he's telling the truth, that is very serious: the governess using her under-age pupil as part of a plan to gradually rob the family of its very important and valuable collection.'

I stirred uneasily. Anne-Marie started to say something, but her eye was caught by her daughter, standing up at her place around the table.

'This is too silly,' she said, standing tall and losing all trace of girlish manner or lack of confidence. 'You followed me the other day, didn't you? I slipped into a dark doorway and saw you driving round and round Bergen's one-way streets. You'd think an ex-policeman could do better than that, wouldn't you? In fact, you were generally a little bit bamboozled. You thought you were following a schoolgirl dressed up as an adult in stuff from her mother's wardrobe, didn't you?'

'Your governess's wardrobe, more like,' said Svein sourly.

'Neither. You see, when I'm in fancy dress is when I'm here, being Daddy's little girl.' She put her hands up to her chin in a girlish gesture and fluttered her eyelids at us. Even Svein realised that while she had been talking she had been growing before our eyes into her real age. 'You see, Daddy has a problem – boy! Does he have a problem! He only fancies little girls. Mummy had me when she was fifteen, though they were married in Thailand and have always lied about her age here. Mummy's problem has been the same as mine: she's grown up. I seem to have gained about a year since I was eleven, though that was six years ago now. Daddy's been so *awfully* careful of me, *so* keen on shielding me from premature adult experience. Pity he didn't realise that Chris and I were discovering an adult relationship he hadn't even considered a danger.'

She stood before us, a young woman in girl's clothing,

a sort of goddess of revenge, her eyes glinting, her face glowing with a long-delayed satisfaction at being who she really was. She went and stood behind Chris, her hands on her shoulders, proudly, and she suddenly gave the impression of being in reality the dominant partner.

'And do you know,' she said, 'just as exciting as finding out who I was and what I wanted, was the knowledge that Chris had done her degree at Middlesborough University on 'The Economics of Art'. All the money side was child's play to her.'

A car drew up outside. Her father got out and strode towards the house. Ingrid left her place and went towards the door. When it opened she threw her arms around her father's neck, a schoolgirl again.

'Hello Daddy! It's lovely to have you home! I'm just telling all the people here about our little games together – all the funny little things you do to me. Of course I know it's always been our own precious secret, but I think most of them could guess, don't you, when I was never allowed to grow up. And of course I had my own little game, that you never guessed about: slipping into your room to get the key to the Munch room at night when you were drunk to the world. This nasty man has accused me and Chris of stealing the Munchs, when really I was only taking payment for all my services rendered. Payment that will finance Chris and my life together.'

She looked at him triumphantly. At the table Anne-Marie's hand was clutching Vidar's. For a moment Fjørtoft's face was absolutely and characteristically blank. Then, unnervingly, he sank to his knees and started to blubber. It was a horrible sound, like a little boy refused a second helping of rømmegraut with currants. Svein watched for a moment, then went over and spoke close to his ear.

'What you do now is up to you. Call the police or hush it up, it's your choice. Hushing it up will be more expensive, but calling the police will be nastier. I shall be sending in my bill, and it will be large.'

Then he beckoned to Semyon and his interpreter and we went through the hallway and out of the front door. In the fresh air the interpreter went straight to the car. Semyon thought for a moment, then went towards the stable. I think the interpreter had been translating all that had been said into Russian, and he sensed he might be on to a good thing.

I stood for a moment or two. The last time I had had a pee had been outside the photocopying shop. I raised my leg beside the door frame and out it came. On and on it went. On and on. My bladder was very full, but I think I was also making an existential statement: the harder you push the plug in on nature, the more it will look for a way to burst exuberantly forth.

I jumped into the front seat of the car and we drove towards town.

The Path to the Shroud

Violetta knew she had made a mistake almost as soon as she got into the shop. She had come in because she noticed a sign saying 'English Books' in the window. English newspapers had been easy to obtain in Parma, books less so. Now she was inside the shop she realised just from casting her eyes around the covers of books on display that she was in a religious bookshop. Not at all what she needed. She was in Italy for experiences, but not for religious ones, or not Christian ones. She dawdled around the pokey interior only to avoid the ungraciousness of walking straight out again.

The face hit her before she even found the section of English books. The sepia image of a bearded man, infinitely kind, unendingly forgiving: the picture of a man (Violetta thought) who grieved for the sufferings and forgave the transgressions of his fellow men – strong, loving, understanding. Who was he? She struggled with the title of the book: *Il Sudario di Torino*. She frowned. Torino she knew. It was one of the places she had put among the possibilities on her itinerary: Turin. Then 'sudario' – but of course! She didn't even need to scrabble in her bag for her pocket dictionary: this must be the face of the man on the Turin Shroud.

She looked again, concentrating on the face. The man seemed to look back, equally intent on her. Again she felt that the eyes of the man *saw,* saw *into,* understood. It was as if her whole life, her rackety, unstructured, uncertain journey through this and that enthusiasm or commitment, was in this man's brain as he gazed at her, and as if his insight gave the whole messy cycle a meaning and a purpose.

'Do you have this book in English?' Violetta asked the woman behind the counter. She shook her head slowly, but went over to the two or three shelves of English books to check. Then she shook her head more decidedly.

'Is not 'ere in Eenglish. In Torino maybe you find.'

'I'm going to Turin,' said Violetta, suddenly definite.

'Turin, yes. You find there per'aps. We 'ave phamplet in four languages. Maybe you like, so you read a little first?'

Violetta took the proffered 'phamplet', and immediately decided to pay the four thousand lire demanded for it. The face was on the front page, and English was one of the four languages, along with French, Spanish and German. She went out into the morning sunlight with a strange feeling of lightness, almost of happiness. She couldn't remember the last time she had felt almost happy.

She didn't look at the pamphlet when she got back to her hotel room. She saved it up. She showered, made herself up as if going to a party, then went back into town and made for the great square in front of the cathedral and baptistery. She walked purposefully across its cobbled expanse to the Angiol d'Oro nestling in the corner. She had been saving up one of the few remaining good restaurants of Parma, and tonight was certainly the night. She had no need of a book to console her loneliness. She watched the other customers, relished the food slowly, and dreamt of the bearded face that had somehow – miraculously? – been preserved on the shroud. She ended with the best gorgonzola she had ever had in her life, relished the last of the wine, then headed back to her hotel.

The pamphlet was still nestling in the big, shabby old bag she always took with her on these exploratory holidays. She took it out, then sat on her bed feeling replete, contented, and above all full of anticipation.

She read the text of the pamphlet first. It was aimed at the faithful – and Violetta had never been that, in any sense. It did not shrink, however, from the findings of modern research. Scientists were of the opinion (they did avoid the word 'proved') that the shroud was in fact of thirteenth- or fourteenth-century provenance, just the period when mentions of this wonderful relic of Christ's death began to be recorded. The image of the man was not made by any conventional paint, stain or other artist's material. Indeed, it seemed that science was unable to suggest what the image consisted of at all, other than with such (unscientific, surely?) images as 'a burst of radiant energy'. That conjecture tickled Violetta's interest almost as much as the face itself. She looked back at the cover.

Violetta was a great frequenter of art galleries – hence

Italy, hence the Italian cities slightly off the usual tourist trail. Her interest in art was amateur but intense. And she could swear that the image of the man on the shroud was like no image of a man in any thirteenth- or fourteenth-century painting. It was too realistic, not stylised enough. This was a man you could touch, imagine embracing. It was like an old sepia photograph of one's great-grandfather as a young or youngish man. Even if the image were of paint, Violetta could not have believed it was made in the thirteenth century.

As it was, it was not of paint; it was made by some substance or process unknown even to modern science, and it was an image startlingly modern in its realism.

Violetta got up and poured herself a whisky from the litre bottle she had had to trail around Parma to find. She had been devastated to discover at Heathrow that duty-free bottles were no longer available to travellers within Europe.

'Bugger the Common Market!' she had shouted at the girl behind the till. Still, she had at last found a supply in Parma, and would get more before moving on, just in case.

Walking around her hotel room, whisky and water in hand, Violetta decided that she was rather pleased the shroud was of medieval material. It removed the religious trappings which roused no resonances in her own mind. It left, though, the image of a medieval man, and the mystery of an image of him projected on to his shroud by no known means. That was exciting.

Violetta had always felt she had a gift for the paranormal, just as she had had a series of flirtations with alternative therapies and folk medicines. Karmas and Eastern thought systems and even simple hypnotism were things that fascinated her, and she had been 'into' many of them with great thoroughness, before passing on to the next enthusiasm. She had no problem with an image, whether of Christ or of some medieval man, projected after death on to the shroud in which his body was wrapped. She definitely preferred the idea of its being a man of the thirteenth or fourteenth century. Christ was a known factor: both the worshipper and the sceptic had a picture of him based on things he did, things he said – or was supposed to have done and said. But the medieval man had mystery: the nature of this figure who lived life so intensely that his image projected itself after death onto his shroud was no problem to absorb for one who had taken spirit manifestations and advice from the great beyond in her stride. Its attraction was that *she* could create him from his image. From the fact, that body, she could mould a figure in whom she could believe.

'A man of Turin,' she said out loud. 'Perhaps the ancestor of a man, even many men, living in Turin today.'

Two whiskies later, as she drifted off into sleep, the image of the man was gaining substance. A man who filled every minute with vitality, experience, passion; one who 'loaded every rift with ore' because he sensed that his life would be short. A man who lived and understood life so completely and intensely would be one who understood others, saw through to their essence, knew and forgave them because life was not for the saints and the mystics and the hermits. It was a messy business for all the rest – people who tried to engage with it totally.

The next day Violetta took the train to Turin. Coming out of the magnificent station she saw the Grand Palace Hotel. Somewhere a little bit grander than she was used to. Somewhere where she might entertain people . . . someone. She walked across, found they had a room vacant, and took it.

That evening she did no more than prowl around the environs of the hotel and station, dropping into a little restaurant for pasta and then swordfish. She read the Terry Pratchett she had brought with her. It would be ostentatious to read about the shroud in Turin itself.

The next day she really set out to explore the city. She walked and walked, her eyes darting everywhere as she fluttered from wide street into spacious square.

Eventually, she knew, she would go and see the shroud. The real thing was on exhibition for millennium year. Normally only a copy was shown, even to the faithful. But the shroud could wait. She skirted the great squares of the old Piedmontese capital, sometimes glancing at the expensive shops, but usually trailing her eyes restlessly from face to face, from besuited business executives to overalled plumbers and builders, from waiters and bus-drivers to tourists in shorts and loud shirts. After an hour or more she sat down at a table in an outdoor cafe on the Piazza Castello.

'Una spremuta d'arancia, per favore,' she told the waiter, after subjecting him to a prolonged but unsatisfactory scrutiny.

Restlessly she resumed her inspection of the townsmen from afar. Absentmindedly she stirred sugar into her *spremuta*. Tasted it – delicious. She sat back in her chair.

Then suddenly she saw him. She would have said to the end of her life, if she had lived long, that an emanation from him came across the huge square from towards the royal palace at the far side and seized her. Perhaps the truth was that he was standing in the middle, and matched from afar the specifications of what she was seeking. Tall, bearded – and even from a distance, she felt sure, magnetic. She slapped notes down on the table and left the cafe, crossing the road, then moved into the main body of the Piazza Castello. Now she could see him from a distance of twenty yards or so, still looking in her direction. Suddenly he turned and walked in the direction of the royal palace. There was no question what Violetta would do. She had already marked it down as one of her sort of places. Now it moved to being a top priority.

She strode ahead, almost running in her eagerness not to lose sight of him – past tourists feeding the birds, past a news stand with a placard reading:

ANCORA UNA DONNA UCCISA.

She gained the entrance to the palace and saw him coming out of the ticket-office-cum-bookshop. Breathless by now, she ran in and again slapped money down. The woman behind the grille told her that a tour started in five minutes. Trying to get her breath back, she stood for a moment outside, under the dark arches that bordered the central courtyard. There was a little knot of people to her left, and cautiously she went over and mingled with them. Almost all seemed to be tourists. But there, among them, he was: tall, solidly built, with the bushy beard and long hair of the shroud giving him the air of a young patriarch. He was half turned away from her, so she could not see his eyes. Then a small woman came along to herd them together, apologising for her poor English, but explaining that in every room there was a notice in three languages explaining the room's contents and purpose. Violetta wondered whether the Man of the Shroud spoke English.

Once they got past the magnificent staircase it was easy to keep close to him. Sometimes she darted up to the notices and ostentatiously read the English text. It was in the third room, the Queen's Reception Room, that he came up behind her and spoke to her.

'You like palaces and such things?'

His voice was soft but urgent, his English heavily accented but seductive. Seductive on a high intellectual and spiritual plane, Violetta decided.

'Very much,' she answered, smiling up at him. Now she could see his eyes, which had a piercing intensity. 'This one is very fine, if maybe a little musty.'

'Musty? What is musty. You hexplain?'

'Musty – well it's old, a bit shabby, decaying a little.'

'Ah, I understand. But it is old. Nothing 'as been done to it for years. The kings of Savoy, they became kings of Hitaly, then kings of nowhere at all. You see?'

'Very well. You speak beautiful English.'

'Not at all. I need a good teacher. So you see, no one 'as lived 'ere for years, for a century and a 'alf. So it become a bit musty, like you say. But full of 'istory.'

'Yes, it's certainly that. Was this king who became King of Italy the one called Victor Emmanuel, or was that later?'

'Italy have two kings called Vittorio Emanuelle, two called Umberto. The wife of the first King Umberto, Queen Margherita, she 'ave a pizza named after her.'

'Oh, of course.'

'The second Umberto, 'e die in exile, and 'e give the shroud to the Cathedral.'

'*Really*? The shroud! . . . Has anyone ever told you that you look like the man in the shroud?'

The man – still she did not know his name – shrugged. 'Some.'

'Plenty of women I should think.'

'Some. Men and women.' He said it distinctly, as if offended.

'I'm sorry. I didn't mean to suggest you were a ladykiller.'

She did not notice his faint start.

'What is that – a lady-what?'

'Ladykiller. It's another word for a Don Juan or a Casanova.'

'Ah – a Casanova. Maybe all Italian men have a little bit of a Casanova in them.'

'Maybe they do . . . Do you live in Turin?'

'Yes – I have a little flat.'

She nearly asked him what a native of Turin was doing going on a conducted tour of one of its monuments with a party of tourists, but she bit the question back.

'It must be a wonderful city to live in.'

'It is very hexciting. It suits me. I live my life fully and eagerly.'

'I'm sure you do!' She said it not flirtatiously but seriously. 'I felt that, too, about the man in the shroud.'

'You did?'

'Scientists who have carbon-dated it say it's not two thousand years old, just six hundred or so. I had the idea, the image of a man of the middle ages or the Renaissance who had lived life to the full, with such energy, such zest . . . Eagerly, like you said.'

'Maybe you are right. Maybe he was my many-greats grandfather.'

They looked at each other and laughed. If she had not been under the spell of the shroud she might have seen that his eyes were cold, that they belied his laugh.

The tour of the royal apartments was coming to an end. They emerged into the courtyard of the palace, then through an arch back to the Piazza Castello. Violetta could see her man for the first time in the sunlight. How strong the mouth was, how bright the eyes! He was even more exciting than she had thought.

'I've been so glad of your company. Could I buy you coffee? Or lunch – it's not far off lunchtime.'

'Alas – I have to go back to my flat, my studio. I am a poor artist. I must get images from the palace into my sketchbook – mere stuff for the tourist trade, you understand, but my living. This hevening. What about dinner this hevening?'

'What a good idea!' said Violetta, at last giving way to her girlish flirtatiousness. 'Why don't you come to my hotel? I believe the Grand's dining room is excellent. Or we could go out to a restaurant.'

The man shook his head.

'I am not a person to call at a respectable hotel. I would

not compromise a fine lady like yourself – me a poor, dirty artist. You come to my flat. I cook you a fine meal, authentic, something handed down in my family for generations.'

'How exciting!'

'I promise you, exciting! Here is my card. You come at eight?'

'Eight o'clock,' she said, looking at the card. 'Mario Pertusi.'

'But you can call me Casanova. The ladykiller.'

They both laughed again. She wished she could kiss him her arrivederci, but she just said it and raised her hand, walking away across the square, past the news stand with its shrieking headline, past the cafes and the banks and the tourist office. Before plunging into the small streets leading to the cathedral she looked round, but her poor eyesight did not allow her to see Mario Pertusi still watching her from the entrance to the Palazzo Madama, his eyes cold and searing, his thin-lipped mouth open in anticipation.

And while Pertusi went back to his studio flat, with its crude drawings of women in notebook after notebook, its worse than amateur attempts at oil-paintings of screaming red mouths, bulging eyes, slashed breasts, which he now turned with practised hand to the wall, Violetta went to the cathedral and the queue to see the shroud, under skies that were clouding over fast. She was told that you had to buy a ticket to see it, and that the ticket office (of course) was elsewhere, back in the Piazza Castello. When she had bought it and taken it back to the cathedral she was told that the ticket was for admittance at a certain time – at seven o'clock that evening, in fact.

'Are you trying to keep the damned thing secret?' she yelled at the scandalised priest on the door, then turned and ran out into the heavy rain which had now been pouring for five minutes. She looked around at the sodden nuns, at the priests with little groups from their villages, the women's groups that bore an awful resemblance to British Women's Institutes. She screwed up her ticket and dropped it on the cathedral steps.

'I don't need to see him,' she said. 'I've seen him.'

She made her way, absurdly happy and at peace, back to the Grand Hotel. She didn't need lunch – couldn't face anything so mundane. In her room she bathed, then lay on her bed dreaming, *seeing* him – the all-forgiving eyes, the air of vast and varied experience, the presence of a man who took on his shoulders the whole burden of sinning humanity.

Soon she sank into a light doze. Then she got up, put on her best and silkiest underclothes, her smartest dress. She emptied her bag to find his card and looked at his address. That was easy enough: a tiny street off the Via dell'Accademia. She could hardly wait, but forced herself to. To drink whisky would be like some kind of profanation. She must have all her senses alert, alive. At last it was time. She skirted the Piazza Carlo Felice till she found the Street of the Academy. At last she found Mario's little road, and number 12. It was an old house, shabby, dirtied by a million Fiats, by the dust and grime of passing humanity. There were no bells on the outside, but plenty of light inside. He had put them on for her. Third floor it had said on the card. She went inside and walked up the stairs, hardly able to contain her excitement. There were two flats on the third floor, one seemingly empty. On the other was the name: MARIO PERTUSI. She waited for one delicious moment.

Then she rang the bell to begin her assignation with her shroud.

Lovely Requiem, Mr Mozart

Mr Mozart, who appeared in two of my 'Bernard Bastable' books, is a historical figure, but one of the 'what if' variety. He is an answer to the question, 'What if Mozart had stayed in Britain after his 1764 visit?' My answer was that he would have been reduced to musical hackwork, writing pap music for pantomimes and vaudevilles, and being patronised by royalty and bigwigs. In the second of the books, when Mozart was in his 70s, he formed a friendship with the young Princess Victoria in whom he was trying to discover some musical talents. Things seemed to be looking up . . .

The commission came into my life accompanied by Mr Lewis Cazalet. The arrival of that gentleman was announced by Jeannie, my unusually bright and alert maid of all duties.

'There's a wee mannikin to see you. Says he has a proposal, something to your advantage.'

I did not jump up with the alacrity I would once have

shown. My position as piano teacher to the Princess Victoria brought me, as well as great pleasure, none of it musical, a great number of prestigious pupils. I stirred reluctantly in my chair, only to have Jeannie say: 'Don't hurry. Let the body wait.'

I nodded, and went to the piano and played a showy piece by my friend Clementi, sufficiently *forte* to penetrate walls. Jeannie came in as I was finishing.

'He's walking up and down. He's a mite . . . unappetising.'

I raised my eyebrows, but I relied on Jeannie's judgement, and told her to show him in.

The gentleman whom she ushered in was not short, but there was a sort of insubstantiality about him: he was thin to the point of meagreness, his gestures were fluttery, and his face was the colour of putty.

'Mr Mozart?' he said, taking my hand limply. 'A great honour. I recognised one of your sonatas, did I not? Your fame is gone out to all lands.'

I was not well disposed towards anyone who could confuse a piece by Clementi with one of my sonatas.

'Mr . . . er?'

'Cazalet, Lewis Cazalet.'

'Ah – a French name,' I said unenthusiastically. That nation had virtually cut the continent of Europe off for twenty years, the very years of my prime, when I could have earned a fortune.

'We are a Huguenot family,' he murmured, as if that was a guarantee of virtue and probity.

'Well, let's get down to business. I believe you have a proposition for me.' We sat down and I looked enquiringly at him.

'Perhaps as a preliminary' – No please! Spare me the preliminaries! – 'I should say that I am a man of letters, but not one favoured by fame and fortune like yourself.' Did my sitting room look as if I was favoured by fortune? 'As a consequence I have been for the last five years librarian and secretary to Mr Isaac Pickles. You know the name?'

I prevaricated.

'I believe I have heard the name mentioned by my son in Wakefield.'

'You would have. A great name in the north. Immensely wealthy. Mr Pickles – his father was Pighills, but no matter – is one of the foremost mill-owners in the Bradford district. He is, in newspaper parlance, a Prince of Industry.'

'I see,' I said. And I did. A loud vulgarian with pots of money and a power lust.

'A most considerate employer, and generous to boot on occasion. I have no complaints whatsoever.'

'That's good to hear. In sending you to see me this, er, Pickles has some end in view, I take it?'

Mr Cazalet hummed and hawed. Then he suddenly blurted out:

'A requiem. He wishes you to write a requiem.'

'Ah. I take it you mean a requiem mass. Is Mr Pickles a Catholic?'

'He is not. His religion is taken from many and is his own alone.'

'And the person for whom this requiem is to be written?'

'Is immaterial.'

'I assure you it is not. If it is for His late Majesty King

George IV it would be very different to what I would write if it was for the Archbishop of Canterbury, for example.'

'I would imagine so!' He hummed again, let out something like a whimper, then said: 'It is a requiem for his wife.'

'I see. Mr Pickles was a devoted husband I take it?'

'Mr Pickles is the complete family man – affectionate, but wise . . . I must insist, however, that the information I have just given you remain completely confidential. Com-plete-ly.'

'It will. But there must surely be a reason for this request?'

He looked at me piteously but I held his gaze.

'The lady in question is still alive.'

I sat back in my chair and simply said 'Phew.'

In the next few minutes he confided in me the facts of the case. The wife in question was sick, sicker than she herself recognised, the doctor was certain her illness was terminal, but would not commit himself to a likely date. All the uncertainties of the commission would be reflected in the fee, and there was one further condition that Mr Pickles absolutely insisted upon:

'That is that you tell no one of this commission, tell no one that you are writing a requiem, tell no one when it is performed that you wrote it, and give total and absolute rights in the work to Mr Pickles, along with all manuscript writings.'

'I see,' I said. 'And the fee he suggests that he pay me?'

'The fee he is willing to pay you is fifteen hundred pounds.'

Fifteen hundred! Riches! Good dinners, fine silk clothes, rich presents for my children and grandchildren. Oh wondrous Pickles!

'Say two thousand,' I said, 'and I am Mr Pickles's to command.'

I was not deceived by the conditions. Mr Pickles was an amateur musician who wanted to pass my work off as his own. When his wife died he wanted to impose on the world by pretending that the superb requiem that was performed for her was written by his good self, divinely inspired (rather as that arch imposter Samuel Taylor Coleridge tries to pretend that his poems were in fact written by the Almighty, with himself acting merely as amanuensis). And it would all be in vain: every society person with any musical knowledge would know it was not by him, and anyone of real discernment would guess it was by Wolfgang Gottlieb Mozart.

The only fly in the ointment was spelt out for me by the Princess Victoria at her next weekly piano lesson, where she murdered the works of lesser men than I (I had learnt the lesson of not encouraging her to her painful operations on works of my own). When she had screwed out of me the reasons for my lightness of heart (unusual, even with her delightful presence) she said:

'He seems a very dishonest man, Mr Mozart.'

'Distinctly devious, my dear.'

'Devious! What a lovely word. If he can rob you of credit for the music, he can hardly be trusted to pay you for it.'

It was something I resolved to bear in mind.

* * *

From the start Mr Pickles showed he had learnt lessons from the negotiations of Mr Cazalet.

'The fee I'm offering,' he said to me in his Hyde Park mansion, 'is two thousand pounds. Subject, naturally, to some safeguards.'

Two thousand pounds, as asked for! I wouldn't like to say how long it would take me to earn that amount by more legitimate pursuits. Kensington Palace paid me thirteen and sixpence an hour for my lessons with the princess. We were sitting on a superb sofa, which must have been in Mr Pickles's family since the time he started to make a fortune from his niche in the cotton industry, which was warm underwear. I could have done with a pair of his long combinations now: this luxurious sofa was about half a mile from the nearest of two fires in the high-ceilinged drawing room of his mansion. I got up and strolled over to his fine grand piano, much nearer the fire. I played a few notes.

'This will need tuning,' I said. Mr Pickles was outraged.

'I assure you it is just as it came from the makers.'

'That is the problem. Pianos go out of tune.'

'But the finest singers and pianists have used it,' he neighed, like a child wailing. 'My musical soirées are famous.'

'Mr Pickles, I played for King George III when he was a young man. I know when a piano needs tuning.'

He backed away at once.

'Yes, yes, of course. But we haven't gone over the cond— the safeguards.'

'For a fee of two thousand pounds I accept those without question. If I understand Mr Cazalet, they are that you will own the piece absolutely, my name will not be attached to it, nor will I verbally lay claim to it. I suggest you might like to call it the Pickles Requiem, and state on the title page that it is "by a gentleman".'

Mr Pickles almost purred.

'Yes, yes. That has a ring to it. "The Pickles Requiem". In memory of my late wife, of course.'

'Of course. I didn't realise that your wife had died since I talked to Mr Cazalet.'

'She has not. I refer to her proper designation when the great work comes to be performed.'

'I see.' (But I didn't).

'I want the piece to be sung within a week of her death, as a direct statement of my grief and sense of loss.'

'Of course, I quite understand . . . You might find it advisable to let the orchestra and choir rehearse as much as possible in advance.'

'Ah yes, I see. Well spoken, Mr Mozart. It must be done in the most tactful way possible.'

'Totally secret, I would suggest. The public prints take any opportunity for ridicule . . . Now I think our business is over?'

'You accept my conditions? And will compose the work entirely in this house, and leave the manuscript and any notes here always?'

'I do accept, and will write the piece as you stipulate.'

We shook hands on it. I had not thought it necessary to mention that nothing in the 'safeguards' prevented me from writing out a second copy at home when I was satisfied with a movement.

On the following evening a message arrived from Pickles Palace (as I called it in my mind) with the news that the Danish couple I had recommended, Herr Bang and Dr Olufson, had been and tuned the piano. No expense spared, obviously. I felt quite sure Mr Pickles noticed no difference.

I began work next day. An anteroom next to the drawing room was assigned entirely to me – the lowly room being chosen not to downgrade my position and purpose in the household but to give easy access to the piano. I say 'began work', but I had begun work on it in my heart before Mr Cazalet had closed the front door. It was to be a work not full of grandeur, still less grandiloquence, with no trace of suffering or hell fire. It was to be gentle, gracious, kind on the ear – a feminine requiem you might say, for the wife of a wealthy industrialist who must surely be his superior in manners, knowledge of the genteel world, and kindness.

On my third day of working in Pickles Palace, when I was just completing the Sanctus, which I had decided to write first, I had the honour of a visit. I was sitting in the great drawing room with welcome spring sunshine coming through the high windows, and trying things over on the piano, which was now a superb instrument and sounding like one. I was conscious after a time that I was not alone. I looked round in the direction of the door towards the hall, and saw a figure standing near the fire.

'Very beautiful, Mr Mozart. Very lovely.'

The voice came as if from a great distance. It was

genteel – no, aristocratic – and it proceeded from a slim, graceful yet commanding woman of perhaps thirty-five or forty, elegantly dressed in a loose-fitting day gown. What a contrast she made to the mighty Pighills himself!

'I am honoured by your approval. Do I have the pleasure of—?'

'Mercy Pickles,' she said, distaste creeping into her tones. 'I hope you will create one of the great ecclesiastical musical works. It should have a life beyond the immediate one marking the death of my husband's mother.'

'Mo—?' I pulled myself up. 'I suppose all composers would like to think their works will last.'

'He is very fond of his mother,' she said, in the same distant tones she had used hitherto. 'She used to make the mill-children's gruel and beat them when they went to sleep. Naturally he's devoted to her, but I found her less than charming.'

'A wife seldom gets on with her husband's mother,' I said.

'When my father sold me, at the age of sixteen, to a man more than twice my age, his mother made it her business to make my life an endless swamp of misery. When she suffered the onset of senility I made it my business to return her treatment in kind. It palled after a time. There was little joy in mistreating someone so far removed from the world that she could not appreciate the fact that she was being mistreated. Now all I wish is that she would hurry up dying.' She stopped, possibly feeling she had said too much. 'And then we can all hear your wonderful requiem.' She thought for a second, then said: 'Take care, Mr Mozart.'

She glided from the room. 'Take care' is a popular form of farewell that sat ill with her aristocratic air. But perhaps she meant it to be taken not as a courtesy but a warning.

My first encounter with the Pickles sons was no less confusing, but even more thought-provoking. I was playing over a first sketch for the *Libera Me* section – a grand, sweeping theme with a hint of yearning – when the doors of the drawing room opened and two young men began a progress across the great expanse of the drawing room, talking loudly. I went on playing. The voices rose to a crescendo. I was intrigued and stopped playing to listen. The voices immediately ceased. I was impressed: they knew enough about music to notice when it stopped. They turned round and saw me.

'You must be Mr Thingummy.'

I waited. I am not a Mr Thingummy.

'Mozart.'

It was the taller of the two. He pronounced it Mo-zart instead of Moat-zart, a deplorable English habit. However I bowed – a reward for a good try. They began over towards me.

'You're the johnny who's teaching my father composition.'

'Well, not—'

'You've got a hard job on your hands. You're starting from scratch.'

'Typical of my father,' came from the shorter boy. 'Wasting our inheritance on futile projects. Who will believe that he wrote it?'

'And who would believe,' chimed in the older boy, 'that he'd lavish all that money and time on a damned librarian?'

'A damned what?' I couldn't stop myself saying.

'Faithful servant and all that. But a piece of *music*? Choirs and solo singers, orchestral johnnies, the whole caboodle. For a book-duster? It should be a case of, when he dies, slipping a ten pound note to his widow.'

'He's not married, Jimmy,' said the other. 'Not at all, if you get me.'

'Well, in that case you're ten pounds to the good.' The pair turned and resumed their marathon.

It was around this point in the execution of the contract that Mr Pickles began to take a more active interest in the progress of my composition. I found one afternoon when I went to play over the day's inspirations that cups and jugs of chocolate had been set out on a small table, and I had no sooner began playing than a footman came in with napkins and biscuits (biscuits are my weakness but the servants so far had not remembered to offer me any), followed a second or two later by Mr Pickles, who sat himself down and – to be fair to him – listened. At the first pause in the playing he called me over.

'Mr Mozart, you must be in need of refreshment.'

I bowed my head briefly, and made my way over. He had poured into my cup some of the fragrant refresher, while pouring himself a cup from the other jug. Made with the finest Brazilian coffee beans, he explained. It was a country with which his mills had strong financial links. The drink was slightly bitter-tasting but acceptable.

'So how is it going, then? Are you well on the way?'

I had the reputation for extreme facility in the writing of my scores. It was a reputation fully justified when it concerned my pieces written to order for members of the aristocracy or the theatre. Still, four weeks for a full-scale requiem was ridiculous.

'I have five movements well advanced, either on paper or in my head,' I said. 'I have fragments of ideas for the other nine sections. Time will tell which are usable.'

'Ah yes. This question of time—'

I was so daring as to interrupt him.

'Great work is not done in days. Remember, sir, I have strong connections with Kensington Palace. If the princess on whom all our hopes turn hears this is a workaday piece that anyone could have written, she will not attend. But if it is a work worthy of Wolfgang Gottlieb Mozart, then she will come if I persuade her, and I will not need to say anything about my participation in the piece.'

'Oh my!' said my patron, as if he could barely comprehend the joyful possibility. 'A magnificent prospect! A wonderful culmination to our mutual collaboration.'

What a mutual collaboration was I could not guess. All we had was a willingness to pay money on one side and an eagerness to accept it on the other, a purely commercial transaction.

So things went on. Now and then Mrs Pickles came in, usually listened for a time, then went out, possibly with a banal compliment, sometimes with a barbed remark about her husband or his family, depending on her mood. The boys (James and Seymour were their names, the second being his mother's family name) came either singly or together, greeted me with 'Hi' or 'Good morning', and sometimes added a sarcastic comment, such as 'Earning your daily crust, eh, Mr Mozart?' I didn't like them. Their father was at least fond of music, even if he knew nothing about it. The boys were simply vessels, without learning or achievement. I heard from the servants that they were both very deep in gambling debts.

The course of my time with the Pickleses changed one afternoon at the beginning of May. I had been forced, on my way out of Pickles Palace, to make a quick visit to the privy, the nature of which I won't go into. I was just washing my hands in the bowl of lukewarm water renewed every hour by a lower footman, when I heard two voices passing along the corridor outside. One was Mr Cazalet, whose work in the library prevented my having much to do with him while I was in the house, and the other was his, and temporarily my, employer, Isaac Pickles.

'The uncertainty is playing on your mind I fear, sir.'

'Oh, I'm perfectly all right. Masterpieces are not made in days, or even months, as Mr Mozart says. But I worry a little about him. He is not a young man. He looks increasingly ill every time I see him.'

'I see him very little,' said Mr Cazalet neutrally.

'Just so long as he lasts long enough to complete the great work,' came Mr Pickles's voice fading down the long corridor. Then I heard him laugh – a silly, childish laugh. I stayed in the privy, frozen to the spot, looking at my reflection in the glass.

I was not looking ill, not 'increasingly ill' every time I

came to the Pickleses. If I was, the princess would have noticed and been concerned. She is very conscious of the great gap between my great age and her little one. She has so few congenial souls around her that she is desperate not to lose one of them. No, I was not looking more and more sickly.

On the other hand, there was the bowel trouble that had taken me to the privy in the first place.

There was another thing that troubled me: the foolish laugh as the pair disappeared from earshot. It sounded not just silly, but less than sane. Senile. And I thought of the fearsome mother now apparently sunk into imbecility for many years. Was senility heritable? Did that explain the multitude of reasons given for the requiem's composition: to me it was for his wife; to his wife it was for his mother; to his thoughtless and senseless sons he gave the least likely explanation of all – that it was for his librarian. It all sounded like a foolish jape. It suggested softening of the brain.

I told all this to the Princess Victoria at the beginning of her next lesson. Her performances that day were more than usually inaccurate and insensitive, and I drew her attention to this several times. Finally, as the lesson ended, she pulled down the piano lid and said: 'I'm sorry to play so badly, Mr Mozart. The truth is, I am worried.'

'Oh dear. Your mother and Sir John again?'

'Not at all. Well yes, they are at it, but it's you I am worried about, and what you told me about Mr Pickles. Has it occurred to you that, if he is so concerned to hide the authorship of this requiem, the most convenient death for him would be your own?'

I fear I was so surprised that I could make no adequate response. I took my leave, made for the door, and turned to bow my farewells. The princess had not finished with me.

'What was the nature of this little room from which you overheard this interesting conversation, Mr Mozart?'

My mouth opened and shut and I scurried out to make my escape.

Arsenic. That's what it was. I wondered at the princess's knowledge of the ways of the criminal world, but then I remembered she had grown up surrounded by plots and conspiracies. Threats on her life (usually involving the Duke of Cumberland, the next in line to the throne) had been the staple of society and newspaper gossip. Arsenic, the poison that is best administered first in small doses, leading up to a fatal dose. Illness of an internal kind is first established, than accepted as the cause of death. Simple.

And who, after all, questions the cause of death of a seventy-nine-year-old man? I was a sitting duck. And my murderer, insultingly enough, was a brain-softened vulgarian from the north of England!

On the next occasion, later that same week, that Mr Pickles came to hear my latest inspirations, I put into action a cunning but simple plan. Standing by the small table with the chocolate already poured out, I remarked to Mr Pickles that the magnificent proportions of the room were remarkably similar to those of St Margaret on the square, one of the churches we had considered for the first performance of the requiem. I suggested he go to the far end of the room to hear how my latest extracts, from the Benedictus, would sound. He was childishly delighted with my proposal. As he walked the length of the room I changed our cups around. The biter bit! I played some of the Benedictus and Mr Pickles expressed his delight: the music penetrated to the far end of the room and was wonderful. We resumed our discussion over chocolate and I looked closely to see if a grimace came over the Pickles face when he tasted it, but I could see nothing.

My next conversation with a member of the Pickles family came two days later. I was sketching a crucial moment in the *Rex Tremendae* when the door to my little anteroom opened and the younger son, Seymour, put his head in.

'I say, Mr Mo-zart.'

'Yes?'

'This requiem you're writing and pretending my Dad did it all – who is it supposed to be *for*? I mean who is it commemorating if that's the right word. Eh? Who is dead?'

'I believe it is to commemorate your mother.'

'Well, she's alive and blooming and if she's ill she's quite unaware of it. And *we'd* – that's Jimmy and me – heard it was for Cazalet the book johnny. Damned unlikely, what? And now I've heard it is for Gran, who is alive but not so you'd notice and there won't be much difference when she finally goes over the finishing line.'

'I couldn't comment. Maybe your father is confused. Many people who have lived exceptionally active lives do get . . . brain-tired earlier than most of us. Or perhaps he has just been joking.'

'Pater doesn't joke. And a requiem's a pretty funny thing to joke about. But you think senility, maybe? I think I ought to talk to a lawyer. He could be declared *non compos*. Stop him throwing his money around.'

'I doubt it. I have seen no signs of it except for the stories about the requiem. His condition would have to be much further advanced before you could start trying to jump into his shoes.'

'I say, you make it sound unpleasant. I mean, I'm deuced concerned—'

I got up and shut the door on him.

A crisis in an affair such as this should not be too long delayed. In a comedy it would come in the third act, with the outcome in the last. Two days after my conversation with Seymour, Isaac Pickles and I had one of our afternoon meetings. We talked first, I explained my aims in the Tuba Mirum, he got up of his own accord and by the time he reached the end of the room the jugs had been shifted round and I was at the piano ready to play and add a sketchy vocal performance as well.

'Enthralling, Mr Mozart,' he said, when he returned to the table. 'You have excelled yourself – as I always say because you always do.' He took up his little jug of chocolate, poured it into his cup, added sugar, stirred, and then took a great, almost a theatrical gulp at it.

It was as if his eyes were trying to pop out of his face with astonishment – he let out a great, flabbergasted yell, then cried out in fear and outrage. As he weakened he bellowed something – a command, a query, a protestation of innocence. I could only assume he had put a hefty dose of arsenic in my chocolate jug, and was now really getting the taste of it for the first time. I ran to the door, but before I got there Seymour had appeared through the door at the room's other end, and before I could shout servants were running into the room from all quarters. When I got back to the table the butler was trying to induce vomiting, others were banging him on the shoulders or trying to put their fingers down his throat. Soon two footmen came with a stretcher and said the doctor had been sent for. He was taken, crying out and retching, to his bedroom. The family physician arrived twenty minutes later. By six o'clock in the evening he was dead. The doctor, though he had not been consulted recently, heard from servants and family Isaac Pickles's complaints about an upset stomach. The lower footman who serviced the privies gave more specific evidence. The doctor signed the certificate. I was left to ponder what in fact had happened.

On the long walk back to my house in Covent Garden I subjected my assumption to detailed scrutiny. Would a man who had just popped a hefty dose of arsenic into my chocolate jug take a first taste of his own chocolate in the form of a massive gulp? I would have thought that, however confident he was of having got the right cup, some primitive form of self-protection would ensure he took a modest sip.

Then again, why would he try to poison me *now*? The requiem was barely half complete in rough form. If he had waited a few months it could have been in the sort of shape that would mean it could be completed by one of my pupils – the dutiful but uninspired Frank Sussman sprang to mind. Certainly Isaac Pickles couldn't complete it himself. By poisoning me at this point he was spoiling all his own plans, mad as they were, by killing the goose that was laying the golden egg. If senility was setting in – and I rather thought it was – it was strongly affecting his judgment and his logic and causing him to act in his own worst interests.

Was there an alternative explanation? The chocolate, on days when Mr Pickles intended honouring me with his company, was put outside the drawing room on an occasional table, the jugs protected by their padded cosies. When Pickles arrived the chocolate was brought in by the footman if one was around, or by the Great Man himself if one was not. Either outside the drawing room or once he'd got in, Mr Pickles added a small amount of arsenic to my jug or my cup. His plan was a very small increase in amount so that my death could be timed to coincide with the completion (or the as-near-as-makes-no-difference completion) of the requiem. He was already anxiously scrutinising my appearance and convincing himself I was looking ill, as in the early stages of the operation I must have been.

Someone knew I was switching the jugs or the cups. Someone knew that, after a certain time, the arsenic was going not to me but to the master of the house instead.

Two days after Pickles's death I received a note from Mr Cazalet 'written at the request of Mrs Pickles' expressing the hope that I would continue with the requiem 'so that it may be ready in the course of time to commemorate the melancholy passing of her husband.' The note did not say that the old conditions no longer applied and I could compose the remaining movements in the comfort of my own house, so I was entitled to assume that the conditions were still in force. I hoped by returning to Pickles Palace I could be in a position to solve the mysteries of its master's death.

The eclaircissement was not slow coming. After three hours spent in composing (initial uneasiness being settled by the glorious business of creation) I went to the drawing room to play through the near-complete section of the Kyrie – with occasional contributions from my own fallible voice. As I drew to a close, the far door was opened and the figure of Mrs Pickles wafted towards me.

'Ah, Mr Mozart. Still gloriously in full flood I'm glad to hear.'

I bowed.

'You do me too much honour.'

'The tenor solo you sang yourself reminded me of the soprano solo in the Benedictus. I suppose that is intentional?'

She looked at me as she spoke. I held her gaze.

'Intentional of course . . . So you have heard some of my compositions for the requiem already – perhaps from the far door?'

'Retreating when my husband came down to test the acoustics – yes.'

'And perhaps at other times taking peeps through the keyhole?'

'Yes. It's rather a large one, conveniently. I could not see you at the piano but I had a good view of the little table and chairs. And of course of the tray, with the jugs under the cosies.'

'I see,' I said, unusually stuck for words.

'As soon as I saw your little manoeuvres with the jugs or the cups I knew that my warning had at last got through to you. My husband was in the grip of vast senile fantasies in which he was recognised as a great composer. I feared the logical outcome of these delusions, and of all the silly games he played in the household over the person to whom it was to be a memorial, would have to be your death . . . But arsenic is a slow-working poison in small doses, and when my husband became your intended victim – because I knew that is what he would have become – I decided to hurry the process up, for reasons I will not go into.'

She looked at me.

'It has worked very well,' I said. 'For both of us.'

'For both of us indeed,' she said. 'I will leave you to your great work. Please remember that if any of this gets out, the first victim of the authorities' suspicions will be yourself. Farewell, Mr Mozart. We shall doubtless meet when the requiem is performed. You will – what do they call this new trick? – *conduct*, will you not? I shall play the afflicted widow to the best of my abilities.'

And that was how my involvement with the Pickleses ended. When, four months later, the requiem was performed at St Margaret's (a church whose vicar went in for the newfangled business of Catholic ritual and costuming) the glorious work was attributed to me, as all would have known in any case, and Mr Pickles's only look-in was as the 'commissioner and dedicatee of the requiem who tragically only lived to hear the first-written movements of the score.' The Princess Victoria was present with her adulterous mother, and though she said she was 'quite prepared to be bored' she had insisted on a place from where she could see the Pickles family, those whom I described in my introduction to the performance as 'his grieving widow and his inconsolable sons' (one of whom had a racing journal hidden inside his word sheet). I also saw the family, both when I spoke at the beginning and at the end of the performance acknowledging the silent (idiotic English habit in a church) expression of enthusiasm. I saw in one of the walled-off family pews a footman put around Mrs Pickles's shoulders a capacious black shawl, preparatory to attending her out to her carriage. There was on his thick-necked, rather brutal face something close to a leer.

Eight months after her husband's death Mrs Pickles was delivered of what was universally accepted to be a daughter of the late Isaac. The London house had been closed up and sold, and Mrs Pickles – in charge of all family affairs until her sons (uncontrollably angry) reached the age of thirty – had moved up north. A year after my last sight of her she had married one of her one-time footmen, now her steward. I hope this time she married for love, though my brief sight of him with her did not suggest it was a wise one.

'He reminds me of Sir John,' said the princess with a

shiver. She was on the whole a forgiving little thing, but she never was able to reconcile herself to her mother's lover. I wondered whether, when she came to be our queen, her reign was going to be a lot less fun than most people were expecting.

Incompatibles

'My Dad loved fairgrounds,' I wrote on a day in 1978, my pen pausing, trembling, before nearly every word. I have never believed in modern inventions that allow you to write faster, to erase your mistakes or first attempts, so that they are lost forever, whereas mine can be pored over by scholars and language students for ever in Boston University's manuscript library of crime fiction, for which I was writing a short account of my life. 'When the first signs of a fairground being set up appeared on the village green of Ormondskirk, Dad's nose would start to twitch, and he would begin to chart what rides there were, and how he and I would prioritise which were the best, which were new, which of the competitive stalls – pigeon-shooting, coconut-shying or whatever – would most likely be winnable and whether the prizes they offered (cut-glass ashtray, novelty china bust of Marilyn Monroe) were worth the cost of competing.

'I don't know why you bother,' said my mother,

lengthening her vowels to a drawl which she had found fascinating in a long-ago English film. 'It's only for children – and only quite young children could be excited by a ride on the dodgems. Philip is well past the fairground stage.'

'I'm not, Mum.'

''Course he's not, you silly b—'

Dad stopped there. He was always courteous to women, even as he mentally consigned them to an inferior level in his personal hell. 'Fairgrounds are for the eternally young – people who can keep within them the magic and mystery of childhood. And people who can dare – can risk the unknown, the dangerous.'

'I always said you should have been a preacher,' said my mother. 'You'd have had them rolling in the aisles, those that were still awake.'

'Silly bitch,' said Dad, thinking we couldn't hear him as he pottered out to the kitchen. 'Does she think I go along with the garbage the ministers churn out every Sunday? Stuff to give us false hopes and dreams, stuff to keep us in our places?'

'I don't know where he gets all those ideas,' said my mother, who probably thought Karl Marx was an American slapstick comedian. 'His people were all Methodists. Of course my family were all C of E to a man, or woman, and they tried to persuade me it was never going to work, marriage to him.'

'Well, whatever it is that's gone wrong,' I said, 'it isn't because Dad is a Methodist.'

'It's because he's an idiot, living in the past,' said my mother bitterly.

And she had a point. I was already quite well read, through my habit of digging deep into the school library and the nearest town's one, and early on I suspected that my father was a creature of the turn of the century, or even earlier. He admired many American writers because he believed that the US was a more democratic and egalitarian country than his own. He would declaim Walt Whitman to me while my mother was out, and he reread all his holdings of Jack London every second year. Of the British writers he liked Arnold Bennett and H.G. Wells. I had progressed to Aldous Huxley and Christopher Isherwood, and felt vastly superior to him in sophistication. At the same time, my love for him burgeoned.

Politically my father invariably voted Communist. The Nottingham Oakwood constituency in which we lived managed to field a Communist candidate every election, who generally got about forty-five votes, except at one election when a candidate called George Windsor was standing, and he got about 250 votes from people who thought they were voting for a member of the royal family. My dad had been a Stalinist in the Thirties, fell out of love with his hero at the time of the Nazi-Soviet pact, then continued to vote Communist into the age of Khrushchev, always protesting it was 'they' who had lost faith, not him. He and I had lots of sharp debates on this topic, and I came to the conclusion that his ideal society was closer akin to *The Wind in the Willows* than to anything in *Das Kapital*. The two of us nearly came to a breach when I declared myself a Christian, but we came through it.

'At least you've become a Baptist,' my dad said, 'not

one of these "Tory party at prayer" lot, or someone who believed in the nonsense of infant baptism.'

'You enrolled me in the Communist Party the day after I was born,' I said mischievously.

'That's quite different,' said my dad, 'and you know it.'

My memories of my parents revolved around their high days and holidays. In retrospect I wondered that we could have functioned as a family, but probably at the time – the Fifties – there were thousands of collapsed marriages, mostly ones which as a rule put up a show of unity, such was the pressure to conform. Our family was different, in that we put up no show.

One of the high days I remember was the occasion of my Grandma Dixon's funeral.

'Left!' shouted my mother, when the steering wheel of the family's Hillman Minx showed signs of turning right. 'You should have gone left for the ring road, you fool,' she spat out. 'We'll be late.'

'Just what I wanted,' replied my dad. 'Everybody should be late for funerals. Modern society has gone mad on them. You'd think life was so wonderful in the West that the afterlife is bound to be an anticlimax. We're going to take the country road and arrive agreeably late, pleading a traffic jam.'

'You'd never hear the last of this if my mother was still alive.'

'Agreed. But the whole point of the journey is that she's not. And you're as pleased as I am that the old bitch is gone.'

This was attested in my memory by so many vitriolic

characterisations of the dead woman by her daughter that there was no denial from the passenger seat.

'At least you're wearing a black tie,' said my mother, grudgingly.

'Ah, so I am. Bought it for old Ken Bradley, CP stalwart, yet lover of all the old habits and traditions. When he went I knew the moment I heard that he would expect a black tie . . . Good to have a bit more wear out of it, and on a happier occasion.'

'Hmmm. You call yourself a Communist but you're really as conservative as the Archbishop of Canterbury.'

And she had a point there too. Christmas was a good example. Christmas always meant a roast chicken for Christmas dinner (eaten at two), though as the Sixties approached it was supplanted by a smallish turkey, which my dad said was 'the same thing'. Cards were sent to neighbours and friends, people they saw nearly every day, and my dad's presents to me were kept a closely guarded secret, but one of them was always a book: Isherwood was still publishing then, and a new hardback was a real luxury, though more often it would be a H.G. Wells because his productivity rendered his output inexhaustible. I thought my father was the last man on earth to find Kipps and Mr Polly funny.

For the rest it was crackers, white wine, and port afterwards, the Queen's broadcast at three o'clock, then a snooze, and then a row about whether my father should do the washing up (he clung to traditional behaviour patterns for the sexes, but usually gave in and, with me, did the gigantic mound of plates and utensils in a gathering atmosphere of grease, grievance and rebellion).

Perhaps surprisingly, Billy Holdsworth was popular in Ormondskirk. He was 'different', people said. Then again he knew everyone, and not just their names, but their histories, their tastes and preferences, their emotional lives. Going through the village was for him the passage from friend to friend, and everyone got their bit of his time.

'Look at him,' said my mother one day, registering his progress from our large bay window. 'You wouldn't think no one can get a word out of him in this house, would you?'

'We both get plenty of words out of him in this house,' I said.

'When he's in that sort of mood,' said Mother, not averse to having it both ways.

As our house became for me little more than a base camp, and as university loomed, the situation between my parents changed slightly. The pair that would be left behind (as I had every intention of leaving them behind) constituted themselves as government and opposition, permanently at odds. What was said had to be contradicted and mulled over in debate. The late Fifties were the declining years of the Age of Macmillan, with the old charlatan arousing contrary instincts in Billy and Doreen, as I had started to call them. One day the prime minister was a fine gentleman of the old school for one of them, and a posturer and a liar for the other. The next day the positions would probably be reversed, with my dad's Communist convictions making not an iota of difference to his stance on anything. 'Granted that the whole set-up is a tawdry sham that will soon be swept away,' he would say, before launching into a paean of praise for Macmillan's landownerly ties with the working man. Doreen liked what she called 'a clean bill emotionally' which meant she didn't like politicians who played around casually, or were popularly reputed to. 'He's a man of principle,' she would say, and fall into a silent fantasy in which she was a glamorous political hostess and he was a young political hopeful. She used that phrase the day the Profumo affair broke. Unfortunately she used it of Mr Profumo himself. 'He's a man of principle,' she said. 'And look at his beautiful wife. I used to love her when she was in films. *Blanche Fury*, *Kind Hearts and Coronets*. You could see her in a coronet. Always the perfect lady . . .'

'Toothy upper-class nag,' said my father. 'No wonder her poor hubby felt the need to play around a bit.'

By this time I was about to go up to Edinburgh University, for a preliminary interview. 'It's nice and far away,' I said to my friends, 'without being the other side of the earth, like Aberdeen.' My intention was to get a holiday job every vacation so I could cut my stays at home to two or three days three times a year during vacations. My resolution was strengthened by the increasingly deranged arguments at home. Granted that every family in Britain was chewing over the facts and fictions of the Profumo affair, my own family's chews were particularly trying, since there was no intention of getting to the facts of the matter, merely the emotional need to score points off the other.

'There's more in this than meets the eye,' my dad would say. 'I expect Macmillan himself is caught up in it.'

'Macmillan himself!' Doreen shrilled. 'You're up the

wall. He's a man of tremendous integrity.'

'He's got about as much integrity as a used car salesman. And then look at his wife, if you can bear to. She's been having it off for years with a Tory MP. Well-known fact.'

Dad had got that fact from a regular at the Lion & Unicorn, an elderly man who took *Private Eye* solely to find out who was sleeping with whom.

'Go on! A woman as ugly as that? You're off your rocker.'

'That's probably what drives Mac to bosomy dolly birds.'

I banged the door on my way out. I had had more than enough of them – eighteen years of it. I was on my way to an interview at the History Department of Edinburgh University, but my parents were too preoccupied with their idiocies to wish me luck.

It was the same when, at summer's end, I left the house to go to Edinburgh, to the poky room in a cold stone house that seemed to me like heaven and the start of a new life. I was, as I passed through the kitchen and out through the back door, privy to a fragment of their current cause of disagreement.

'It was Newcastle-upon-Tyne,' my father was saying. 'It started with a penny stall in the market there.'

'You're off your head,' my mother said. 'It was a stall, but it was in Nottingham.'

'You're confusing it with Boots, you silly—'

As always my father pulled himself up when the general nature of the word he was about to utter was obvious to all his listeners. I as always banged the door. It was the only way to make them aware of my existence. I walked to the bus stop, my mind full of the journey to Edinburgh, and a whole three months (at the least) away from my irritating (when they were not boring) father and mother. Heaven!

It didn't work out like that. I was no sooner arranging my little store of 'things' in that paradisal Edinburgh room next morning when there was a banging on the front door, and a reluctant unchaining and unlocking of it by my landlady. As I was setting down to my task, conscious of knowing nobody in Auld Reekie, I heard my name. When the two policemen came into the room I said the only thing that occurred to me.

'It's my mum and dad, isn't it?'

And that was my first encounter with murder, which I've built my life around and made my living from. It was horrible, but I was conscious all the time that I was excited as well. And there was, hanging over it, as it hung over all my parents' sayings and doings, the ridiculous.

The neighbour caught it well. He'd come in with some late tomatoes from his market garden.

'Cooee!' he shouted. 'It's only me.'

He heard from the living room the voice of my father.

'You'd think, wouldn't you, with the whole country in a state of uproar and confusion, all politics stood up its head, that we could occupy our time better than arguing about where Marks and Spencer's had their beginnings.'

'If you weren't such a daft idjit,' came my mother's voice, 'you'd know what every household in Britain knows: that it was Nottingham.'

There was silence. Then suddenly a loud, sickening thud.

'I knew they never got on,' the neighbour said. 'Everyone knew that. But I never expected it to come to this. And I'd always admired that big copper preserving pan hanging near the fireplace.'

The business took three days, but it was police bureaucracy rather than any fancy detection that held things up. What had happened in the house called home was all clear enough. I got leave from my new university for a week, and they even helped me to find a new and better room when I returned. The landlady wasn't going to have anything to do with someone involved in a murder.

I often wish I could have had the same cut-out option myself. Every time my name or one of my books comes up in a paper, local or national, there has to be something about the murder in our family. Even as I am writing this, in 1978, seventeen years after the crime, the word murder hangs around me, puts his scaly fingers on everything I'm involved in. It was a murder that sprang out of triviality, and I seem to have inherited the family's gift for it. As I finish my account of the episode I shall look at my watch, stand up, then rummage in my wardrobe to find something suitable for my next appointment. My uncertainty would have been just the same if the killer had been the killed, and the killed the killer. What does the well-dressed crime writer wear to visit a parent in an institution for the criminally insane?

Time for a Change

'It's so damned unfair,' protested Les, sounding as if he was a lawyer, in court, conducting his own case. 'They look at your address and put you in the appropriate school for that area. No appeal worth bothering about against the judgement: the kids from a good area get a good school, and the ones from a not-so-nice area get a not-so-nice school.'

'You don't have to talk to the gallery,' said his father-in-law. 'I spent my life teaching in a good school, as you very well know, but if I tried to get my grandchildren there on the strength of it they'd snigger at me. I only wish I could help, but you know that I—'

'We know, Dad,' said Miriam. 'We understand.'

Ten years before, her father might have helped his daughter to finance a move to a prosperous area, with well-thought-of schools – his own school, for example, where he had finished up as Deputy Head of English. Now the credit crunch and some crass investments recommended by a friend who knew even less about the stockmarket than Ernest Craven meant that help to make that longed-for step up the social ladder was out of the question.

'We can't help finance a move,' said Win, Miriam's mother, 'but we could go in for a swap.'

There was a sudden silence. Miriam was sure this had come spontaneously out, was not something that her parents had thought of before. Nor Les, come to that. If he'd thought of it they'd have discussed it. Now she saw his blue eyes, underneath the floppy lock of blond hair, were sparkling.

'If only,' he said, hesitatingly, his voice breaking.

'I don't see that there's any "if only",' said Win. 'We always liked your house, and there'd be much less housework for me than I have in this old barn.'

'We'll think about it,' said Ernest, sounding as if he was summing up the respective merits of Keats and Shelley at the end of a lesson with 4A. 'Come round on Friday. We'll give you all your teas and we'll talk it over.'

'I really did think of it as "if only",' said Les on the drive home. 'I didn't think of it as a serious proposition.'

'I know, I know,' said Miriam. 'But Dad would have slapped you down if he'd been totally against it. You get on well enough now for him to be perfectly honest with you.'

Yes, Les thought: at least that had been put behind them. Ten years ago, the engagement and the months after it had been punctuated by a typical schoolmaster's cry: 'He's not good enough for you.' Modified later by: 'I don't mean socially, not *class*. I mean intellectually. He'll never get anywhere with a second-rate brain like that.'

Miriam had remained silent, only on one fraught occasion saying that there were many different sorts of brain, and therefore many different sorts of first-rate brains. She battled valiantly for her side of the argument, and eventually Ernest came round to see that for once he had to give in. He had been faithful to a silent vow he had made, and had never mentioned Les's brain since giving them his blessing.

When the younger generation came round for their high teas, Les and Miriam found the matter was virtually settled. They were not a bit surprised: jumping the gun when a decision was in the offing and making it all on his own was one of Ernest's ways of keeping in charge. Now he asked the children first, and got an enthusiastic endorsement of the idea that every child should have a bedroom to itself. Ricky added that he knew the boys in the area, and they were rotten at football, something he seemed to see as a plus rather than a minus. Cathy said that her grandparents' house was like a palace and she was going to study Fine Arts at St Andrew's University where, she clearly thought, some shade of Prince William would inspire her.

Win said she wouldn't bat an eyelid at the fall in social status – only silly people gave it a second thought, she said. Ernest said that as far as he was concerned education was in the top three considerations in life, and if he could help his grandchildren get a better life through better and wiser teaching, that would be worth any sacrifice on his and Win's part.

Les and Miriam didn't need to say anything. The swap was voted on and passed *nem con*, as Ernest roundly pronounced.

The next problem was understanding the system, and making it work to their advantage. Here Ernest's experience as a teacher – and a teacher at one of the schools concerned – was immensely valuable. It was too late in the school year to apply for a place in the normal way. Ricky was ten, and would be eleven by the beginning of the school year in September. Places were filled at Saint Ethelinda's School, apart from a few places kept back to cover emergencies or exceptional late applications.

The committee sitting on the applications consisted of the school's headmaster (new since Ernest's time as English teacher there), a local councillor and a prominent parent. They interviewed the boy's father first, and Les was sure he was not going to distinguish himself. In all his jobs he had impressed by his work ethic and his happy-go-lucky attitude to life and its challenges, so he knew what he said would be vacuous and very little to the point.

'Oh, Ricky's just crazy to go to the school his grandfather taught at. And quite right too. He knows his grandfather was head of English, and English is very much one of his subjects. He knows my father-in-law was Deputy Head by the time he retired, and he's proud of that. They make a wonderful pair, and he'll be devastated if he doesn't get a place. In fact they both will.'

'That's as maybe,' said the headmaster, a punctilious man, 'but at the moment you are not residents of the catchment area of Saint Ethelinda's.'

'Will be by Saturday,' said Les, grinning attractively and

pushing back his fair lock of hair.

'By exchanging houses with your in-laws, I believe.'

'Yes. Nothing wrong with that, is there? We've been thinking about it for years.'

'Could I ask who the boy's grandfather is?' said the local councillor.

'Ernest Craven. Ernie C to the boys in my time.' If a thaw could be visible, this one would proclaim itself with all the self-congratulation of a washing powder ad.

'Oh, a wonderful teacher,' said the parent. 'Couldn't be better. The name is its own guarantee.'

Les agreed, and sat back contentedly in his chair unusually pleased with himself. The work was done even before Ernest was called.

He came in, hand outstretched, to shake the headmaster's hand first.

'Glad to meet you at last. Congratulations. You're doing a fine job. Going fast, but not too fast. Boys don't like wholesale changes. Still, I expect they all like the opening of the sixth form to girls. Or do we say young ladies?'

He turned to the councillor.

'Frank. Good to see you again. I've followed your local successes with interest. Westminster next, I believe? Good show. A firm local base is what an MP needs. And Charlie.' He turned to the parent. 'Producing sprigs for your old school. Good show. I hope your present sprig reads English verse better than his old dad used to.'

Charlie's smile of 'welcome back' was as warm as the councillor's had been. People like to have their weak spots remembered almost as much as their seventy-five runs against Chelmsford Grammar in 1973. The headmaster gave up his predilection for following the rules to the letter. He smiled during the brief interview almost non-stop, and as Ernest was going out said: 'We look forward to welcoming young Ricky to St Ethelinda.' The whole family drank a toast to the headmaster that evening.

The days between the interview and the move were jam-packed with activity. A removalist had been hired for Saturday at 8 a.m. and he was just taking the larger things: the dining table, the double bed, the piano that was a historical monument to Ernest's efforts to make the young Miriam musical. After these things had been removed from one house to another each family had hired a smaller van and had lined up friends – Ernest's bowls mate Kieran, Les's friend Harry from the insurance firm they both worked for – to take the smaller things: the chests of drawers, the occasional tables, the arm chairs. When they had been taken the ordinary detritus of family living was moved from one house to another and the move was complete.

'Whoops!' said Ernest as they settled down to an enormous urn of tea in the Victorian terrace house they'd taken over from his daughter and son-in-law. 'Forgot the attic.'

'Oh Dad!' said Miriam. 'Forget the attic. It's only rubbish and you won't have looked at some of it for years.'

'Not all of it,' said her father. 'There's . . . a novel. Or the material for a novel. They say everyone has a novel inside them, don't they? Something they long to get down on paper. I'll just down this cuppa, then I'll take the van and go and get it.'

'Well, I'm coming with you,' said Miriam, taking a swift

swig at her mug.

'If you must,' said Ernest, grimly. 'I thought you wanted a rest.'

'I want to see our new house,' she replied. '*Ours* because of your and Mum's generosity. I want to see how my old furniture fits into it.'

'Take him away, for goodness sake,' said Win. 'And don't talk about generosity: this house will be a rest cure after it.'

Father and daughter went to the front door, and got into the two seats of the van. As they sped on the twenty minute drive Miriam could discern – or thought she could – an excitement in her father: a tensed-up yet happy ebullience. You old goat, she thought, giggling to herself. It was bound to be a novel about his teenage sex with someone or other.

Then suddenly she felt a change to sadness for the poor old man who had always been the object of love and respect for her: a novel, written years ago, by a man now well into retirement. It didn't seem as if it was a piece of fiction that had any sort of future. Even if it wasn't an old goat's memories, even if it was a dour memory-play about habits and attitudes in post-war Leeds, its future, if it had any, was as a treasure trove of provincial *mores*. Miriam hoped against hope he never asked her to read it and tell him what she thought of it.

Miriam put the thoughts from her as they arrived at the house. She jumped out of the van and ran up to put the key of the door for the first time in the lock. She went straight into the living room and looked, enchanted, around. She turned to her father. 'Oh look, Dad. I know it's just chance, but they've put that armchair, *my* armchair, just where I want it.'

'You might change your mind come next winter,' said Ernest, still slightly grumpy. 'It'll be too far away from the gas fire.'

'Oh, and the piano. I thought we could slip it into that alcove. I just hope neither of the kids will want to take it up, with all that awful practising. Put away over there they won't even think of it.'

'You'll have fun getting the place how you like it,' her father said, relaxing from his negative thoughts. 'Now, I'll just go and get the box and I'll be off back to Kieran, Win and Les.'

'Dad, let me go up and get it. That attic is—'

'No, no. I know exactly where it is. I'll recognise it. You amuse yourself with your new doll's house.'

And Miriam turned back to look at the room, only slightly worried, because her father had always been a very fit man.

The attic was reached through a square hatch, and Miriam heard her father bringing down the attic's rickety old ladder of rope and wood, secured to the floor inside the hatch. Then she heard him go up step by step, carefully. She went over to the window, thoughts going through her mind about some kind of marriage between the trees in the parkland opposite and the wall in the house's largest room that looked directly out on to it. 'Got it,' she heard her father say triumphantly. It never occurred to her to wonder how large the box was, and whether he would still have an arm left to steady himself with when he came down the ladder.

She was brought up suddenly by a shout – not a scream, but the sort of shout a schoolmaster inevitably had to use at times. She threw open the living room door, then dashed up the stairs and on to the landing where the hatch was. Ernest was lying still on the floor, his left ankle still trapped in one of the lower steps of the ladder. Miriam rushed over and released it, then knelt and felt her father's pulse. She had been a schoolteacher before her own children came along, and she knew all the basics of first aid.

'Oh Dad. You *silly* old fool. Why wouldn't you let me fetch your precious box? I'm ringing for an ambulance now. Love you, Dad . . . Always.'

The ambulance took only ten minutes, but it was the longest ten minutes of her life. She wanted to ring Les and tell him, but she thought he would be taking Kieran home, so she waited until she and her father were in the ambulance, she on a little tip-up seat, her father lying flat out, attached to various dials and indicators.

'Les, darling. Dad has had some kind of stroke or heart attack. I'll be at the hospital when you're free. Could you get your mum to take the children for a bit? And ring my mother and tell her. She'll want to be at the hospital with him. Ring for a taxi for her, or bring her yourself . . . Of course I trust you. Love you too.'

The next two hours were almost unbearable, especially after they were told by the specialist that things didn't look good. Her mother arrived with Les, though the latter stayed only twenty minutes then decided he ought to be with the children. Les's one weakness was a fit person's horror of illness. Win said all the things people do say at such times, and did all the useless things people do except worrying about the state of her husband's underclothes. When the inevitable had happened and the nurse had tenderly shut his eyes, Win demanded to go home to her new home, and asked to be left alone.

'I've got things I want to say to him,' she said. 'I'll be all right in the morning.'

Miriam went to her new home after she had seen her mother safely into her old one. The space in the new house now seemed less of an attraction, more of a disorientating threat. She went up to the landing and looked around. The specialist had said it seemed unlikely there would need to be an inquest. Ernest had had a couple of minor heart scares soon after retirement. Apart from the rickety old ladder, the landing was tidy. The box, the container of all that youthful attempt at fiction, had skidded over to the doorway of the main bedroom, but it had remained intact, the box being secured by a liberal application of freezer tape. The neat package looked faintly pathetic.

'Poor Dad,' thought Miriam. 'He'd never have completed it. The Dad of today was probably a quite different person to the Dad who wrote this.'

She rummaged in her handbag and found a pair of nail-scissors which, with protest, allowed her to attack the sticky tape and open the box. There in four neat little piles, were the handwritten pages of what looked like a series of letters. Miriam went into the main bedroom, where the light was better. She took what seemed to be the first letter

– the opening to the novel she supposed; it had no date on it, nor even any name for the fictional recipient of the letter. '*My dear boy*' it began:

> *I can't tell you how happy you made me today. The assurance that you felt the same attraction to me, had felt it for a long time, made my heart leap for joy. Your feelings betray a maturity beyond your youth. But do remember that our feelings are ones that could easily be misinterpreted. They are our secret, and that is how it must remain.*

Miriam frowned. This was not quite what she had expected. She flicked ahead through the first pile of letters. 'My dearest boy', 'Dear lad', 'My best love', 'My own one' – these were the superscriptions. The events did not seem to progress in the orderly manner of a novel. 'I love your bright eyes, the sight of your delicious, unruly fair hair.' Why should her father be writing a homosexual novel? She had never for a moment suspected her father of nourishing such thoughts. Was it some kind of crime novel, where the reader is offered information but in a way calculated to mislead?

Eventually the awful, inevitable thought struck her. This was not a novel. This was her father, writing himself, writing personally. It was a correspondence of which he had kept only the one side – his own. These were his own real, deeply-felt thoughts. She began to sweat with embarrassment. She took up the second pile. The tone of the top letter was very much that of the earlier ones.

My beloved boy,

As always our games yesterday – so private and perfect, such lovely recreations for both our bodies – were wonderfully perfect and satisfying. How happy the last few years have made me. These letters are my 'thank you', without which the fun and satisfaction would not be complete.

Miriam's eyes were awash. She could not rid herself of the feeling that only in this relationship had her father had real joy and fulfilment. It made her feel that his had been a life misused, only half satisfying. The combination of love and school-masterliness in the tone of the letters only added to this feeling.

She wiped her eyes and burrowed for the very last letter.

My dear, still dear, boy,

I cannot tell you the pain I suffered when I read your last and found that you feel it is time, now you are leaving school, to take up a new sort of relationship. Never before have you told me that what we have had was not enough for you. But I must not reproach you – you who have given me so much. I must wish you well and let you go. Please remember how dangerous this love has been, particularly for me. Please, please, Leslie: pack up the letters securely and return them to me. Those letters would be the end of my career, perhaps of my life . . .

Miriam found she could read no more. Now it all became clear: why her father had opposed so vigorously her marriage, why he and Leslie (Ernest was the only man who used his full name) had never, in spite of having so much in common, come fully to trust each other. She understood the pain he must have felt, seeing his lover as the lover of his daughter, but felt painfully that her father had not done himself justice in that last letter, while Les had had to take hard decisions for his father-in-law's sake, and had loyally stuck to them, however painful his silence must have been for him.

She went into the kitchen, into the muddle of cupboards and drawers, and found her own roll of freezer tape. The box must be the basis of the first garden bonfire in the new house. It would represent for her a thorough and complete destruction of the most important relationship in her father's life. But it was what he would have wanted.

A Slow Way to Di

There was no question about when the wedding day would be: it had to be July 29th 1981. Both David and Julia were agreed about that – had hardly, indeed, needed to discuss it. And when the vicar demurred they presented a united front.

'But nobody will turn up,' he protested.

'Oh but they will,' they chorused.

'Everyone wants to watch the royal wedding,' he countered (he wanted to watch it himself). 'You'll find that a lot of the guests will simply stay away, or trump up an excuse.'

'They won't, because they'll want to watch it on the giant screen at the reception,' David said complacently. 'That's going to be the big pulling point. Oh, and we want the wedding early – nine o'clock.'

'Nine o'clock?'

'That's right. Then the reception can start round about

ten, and we can follow the day through. Oh, people will come all right: two weddings for the price of one.'

The vicar did not like it at all, but his congregation at St Michael's included all too few young people, so he was unwilling to antagonise two of them. And he certainly had to admit afterwards that he had been wrong. So many near-friends and business contacts angled for invitations that in the end Julia's father was persuaded to hire a second marquee. Even the vicar was cajoled into watching the coach procession to St Paul's with David and Julia and their guests, though he was steadfast in his determination to slip away and watch the actual service in the more dignified privacy of his vicarage.

Julia made a pretty bride. Not lovely, not stunning – but then she was not going into this in a spirit of competition. She could sit in the central position at top table and watch the nation's bride and her heart would seem to stop at the beauty of her, just as everyone else's did. Somehow she seemed herself to be part of that beauty. David was, if anything, rather better-looking than the Prince of Wales, but who bothered to look at the bridegroom at a wedding? The age difference between him and Julia was only eight years, but the fact that there was one, and that people commented on it, made a further bond between them and the royal couple.

That bond had been formed when David had proposed to Julia on a brief holiday in Brighton. They had got back to their hotel, holding hands and very happy, to find that the royal engagement had been officially announced to the nation. 'They can't be any happier than we are,' said

David, as they sat on the bed and watched the TV screen. The bond was further strengthened at the reception, when the best man, taking advantage of one of the hiatuses in the television coverage when nothing much was happening, talked (his speech somewhat slurred) of 'the nation's sweetheart' and 'the queen of our hearts here in Beckersley'. Bonds – that was what that day was all about: forming bonds.

That night, which was admittedly no first for them, David rolled over on the bed and said:

'It couldn't have been more wonderful. Everything was perfect. I hope it's been just as good for *them*.'

No one could deny they made a lovely couple. The congregation of St Michael's all said so, and so did their colleagues at their various workplaces. Quite soon they became something special in the small town of Beckersley. They were people who were pointed to, with an odd sort of pride. When the marriage was blessed with children, people's happiness was in an indefinable way crowned, and they smiled knowingly. It didn't matter that the first child was a girl.

'We wouldn't want to be a carbon copy,' said David, when people commented. 'We love her for what she is, and I'm sure they do the same for William.'

It was nice, though, when the second child was a boy. Both parents had an obscure feeling that David had to have an heir.

Of course those years had their downs as well as their ups. David was the more serious of the pair, the more intense. He liked going to plays and art exhibitions, and sometimes he taxed Julia's powers of concentration. Julia was a wonderful mother, as everyone recognised, but her tastes ran more to parties and dancing, and she took a lot of time over her appearance, feeling she owed that to all those people for whom she was something a little special. David didn't resent this. In fact he gloried in it, often remarking that he felt it an honour to play second fiddle to such a wonderful woman. He was rather pleased, though, when she bought a tape of Grieg's Piano Concerto and played it on her Walkman when she was out shopping with the little ones. It showed she had a serious side, he said, which would strengthen and mature with the years.

When did it start to go wrong? People often asked that, in hurt and bewildered tones, in later years.

'It was after the birth of Edward,' David used to say. 'Somehow things started falling apart then.'

Nobody noticed that at the time, though. Some suggested he was using the benefit of hindsight, even making it up to form one further link in the chain that bound them to the royal couple. It was only later that David's workmates at the building society and Julia's young mother friends began to notice telltale signs of disharmony. This was after the newspapers began to have stories of eating disorders, rows, duties pursued separately rather than together, birthdays spent apart. Julia certainly had no trouble with anorexia or bulimia. She had always eaten heartily, and continued to do so. Still, David was out alone more often: not so much at the pub, though he enjoyed the occasional pint with friends, but at the theatre in nearby Peterborough, at meetings on conservation matters, at adult education classes. Julia insisted on a quid pro quo, and David babysat the children while she had strenuous sessions at her favourite gym, or went with friends to London, to the latest Andrew Lloyd Webber piece.

'You don't have to be in each other's pockets the whole time,' she said. 'That's not my idea of marriage.'

Probably the people who knew best how badly things were going wrong were the children, though they *knew* rather than understood. Marina was later to say that her parents were together physically in the spick and span new Barrett home where they lived, but that she always thought of them as apart. Colleagues at the building society where David worked commented under their breath that he mentioned his wife less frequently than he used to. Comment even became malicious, because public taste is fickle and sentimental affection can turn sour.

'I think Princess Julia is in for a nasty shock,' said an elderly worshipper at St Michael's. 'Her prince is going to move out.'

That happened, in fact, a few months before the prime minister announced the 'amicable' royal split. It certainly wasn't a nasty shock, though, for Julia. She had seen it coming for some time, and it came as a relief and a release.

'I'm fed up with him moping and emoting around the house the whole time,' she told her father. 'Now I'll have a bit of space to myself.'

'Is he having an affair?' her father asked.

Julia shrugged.

'Not as far as I know. Good luck to her if he is. At least I can be more open now.'

Julia's father didn't ask her what she meant by that. Over the years he had become just a little in awe of his daughter.

They sold the house and split the proceeds and the property. Julia got a job in a dress shop in Peterborough and bought a small flat for herself and the children. David stayed on in Beckersley, first living with his parents, then, when he had his priorities sorted out, renting a glorified bedsitter. He had an affair or two, mostly with older women, but none of them worked out.

'He's too neurotic,' one of them said later. 'Too driven. Sometimes it was as if I wasn't there.'

Certainly the divorce went through a very bad patch. For a long time they communicated by note, arranging times for him to take the children out by faxes from his office to her shop. When he had taken them to the cinema, the pleasure park or the zoo, he would leave them at the main door of the little apartment building where they lived, never on any account going up the stairs with them to the first floor flat.

This went on for a long time – several years. Then one day, due to a misunderstanding caused by a fax machine which said it had transmitted a page when it hadn't, both turned up at Marina's school's parents' day. It was touch and go when they saw each other. David certainly wished he could turn on his heels and march out of the gate. But in the end a sense of what was expected of them both saved the day. He went over, put his hands on Julia's shoulders, and kissed her on the cheek. They talked for several minutes, and later sat together for the little play the children put on.

'In our position you can't always do what you want,' said David later to his mother.

So after that things went better. They talked when necessary on the phone, met when David picked up the children, borrowed books or tapes that the other had taken when possessions were divided up (David had taken the Grieg then, but he lent her the Tchaikovsky at this period and she said she enjoyed it). The children were pleased at developments, and their parents were not unhappy.

But David had difficulty with the fact that Julia had boyfriends. She never considered marriage again, and the affairs were usually of short duration, because she was happiest on her own. But boyfriends she did have from time to time, and David confided in a colleague at work how hard he found it to cope with the idea.

'It's not the thought of her sleeping with other men,' he said. 'Not as such. It's the feeling that she's letting everyone down and it's not the done thing.'

His colleague refrained from mentioning the widow and the married women David had been involved with, but later he said to his wife:

'Basically he thinks it's *lèse majesté*. The king's wife sleeping with another man commits treason. I expect he'd like to do to her what Henry VIII did to Anne Boleyn.'

'You're just jealous,' said his wife. 'He's got his head screwed on better than that. You can't stomach his leapfrogging over you at work.'

And David was indeed doing very well at the building society. Renting that bedsitter meant he had money to spend on things that impressed people: Italian suits, good restaurants, a fast car. There was an awful moment, or awful few months, when the society was merging with another and converting to a limited company. Branches were to be closed, redundancies were in the air, and it looked as though David, high up though he was, was one of those whose services were to be dispensed with. But he put on a furious display of energy, showed everyone the brilliance of his financial judgment, and put the new company in his debt by saving it from some very bad policy decisions. When the new organisation was finally launched he was one of its deputy chiefs, and everyone agreed that the only way for him was up. But his best friend at work said there was still something withdrawn about him, still something driven and intense.

That was how things stood in the summer of '97. The children were growing up, and he didn't 'take them out' any longer. But he had a fine new apartment in a converted Victorian industrialist's house, and one or other of the children was calling on him all the time, to ask his advice, get him to help financially with something 'everyone else' had at school, or just to chat. He would have liked to ask about their mother and her doings but he was too much the reserved Englishman, and anything they told him in the course of their conversations was marginal or trivial. The fact that Marina and Edward were growing up, starting to lead their own lives, meant he saw Julia even less.

So when, in the early morning of September 1st 1997, Julia was wakened by the sound of gravel on glass, the last person she thought of was David. As a matter of fact she had heard that sound before – the summons of a long-ago boyfriend to leave the family home on warm summer nights – and for a moment it really took her back. She slipped out of bed, then pattered through the hallway and living room to the kitchen. The window opened easily and she looked down towards the gravel path under the bedroom.

'David! What on earth do you think you're doing?'

He turned and came over towards her. Her hand switched on the kitchen light, and as he looked up at her, her first thought was that he looked ill, her second that he was distraught. His face was red, and behind his glasses his eyes looked puffy.

'Julia, I've got to talk to you.'

'Talk to me? At this time of night? . . . What time is it?'

'About half past four.'

'You must be out of your mind.'

'No Julia, it's important. We've got to talk.'

'We are talking. And probably all the neighbours are listening.'

'No they're not. Nobody's stirred. But we can't talk like this. Come down and we can sit in the car.'

His eyes strayed towards his smart black BMW some yards away on the road.

'David, we've been divorced for five years. What on earth can we have to talk about sitting in your car in the road in the middle of the night?'

'I tell you, this is important. You haven't heard, have you? I'll tell you in the car. This is the most important thing that's ever happened to us.'

Julia caught a glint in his eye, reflecting the light from

the kitchen. She thought that, if she hadn't known him better, she might have guessed that he was mad.

'"Us" doesn't exist,' she said brutally. 'It did, it was good for a time, then less good, then nothing at all. Now it's less than nothing.'

'But it isn't. We've still got . . . bonds. Still got responsibilities.'

'The children. And even them we won't have for long.'

'Julia, I can't talk about it like this. Come down, we'll go for a little drive, and then you'll understand.'

'A little drive? In my nightie? Not on your life!'

'Julia, this is something so . . . so big, so awesome . . . You've got to come down so I can explain.'

'I'm surprised you haven't said that it's bigger than both of us.'

David's face screwed up in distress.

'Don't be like that, Julia – not satirical and bitter, not at a time like this. It *is* bigger than both of us. That's exactly it.'

'Fax me about it in the morning, eh?'

His face twisted in anger.

'You've always had a trivial mind, do you know that? You've always failed to live up to your position.'

'My position?'

'Your destiny. I shouldn't be surprised that you're falling so far beneath it now.'

'David, all I want now is my bed.'

'That's because you don't understand.' His voice took on a pleading tone. 'Come down, we'll go for a drive, and I'll *make* you understand what's got to happen.'

She was genuinely bewildered.

'*Got* to happen?'

'Yes. What . . . what all this has been leading up to.'

'It's not up to us to say what's got to happen.'

'Of course it is. You'll see why when I tell you what's happened.'

'What's happened? Have you done anything silly, David?'

His voice rose in exasperation.

'Of course I haven't! It's not a question of what I've done.'

'Keep quiet. You'll waken the children.'

'The children are at your parents' for the last week of the holiday, as you very well know. You're trying to get rid of me.'

'All right David, I'm trying to get rid of you. I've had enough of this, and I'm going back to bed.'

She started to close the window, and as she fumbled with the latch she heard David cry: 'No, don't do that, Julia. Come down and listen to what I've got to say.'

Julia sat at the kitchen table and took out a cigarette from the packet lying there. 'Silly bugger,' she said to herself. 'Anybody'd think he'd gone soft in the head.'

In the silence his voice, more distant now, came to her, still anguished.

'You've failed, Julia. You've been through a test, and you've failed. You're an icon with feet of clay. You'll never realise the greatness that's in you.'

Julia puffed out a neat ring of smoke: whatever were the neighbours going to say in the morning? Silly really, that she still cared what people said about her. At least in this case it was an ex-husband they'd be talking about, not a lover.

She heard with relief a car door slam, then the sound of tyres screaming on tarmac. It was five o'clock. She wondered whether to turn on the radio and try to find a news summary, but decided not to bother. As she went back towards the bedroom she heard a dull boom in the distance. Probably thunder, she thought, though she hadn't sensed a storm in the air. She slipped into bed, lay back luxuriously, then let her hands play over the smooth olive skin of Mehmet, the young man from the kebab takeaway who had delivered her order five nights ago and had been with her pretty well continuously ever since.

The trouble with David, she thought, is that he goes the whole hog with everything. Just so far and no further, that was Julia's motto.

Last Day of the Hols

Miss Trim, the English teacher and form mistress of 6A, looked around at the eleven year olds staring stolidly back at her. 'The essay topic for your Easter break,' she said, then paused solemnly. She had begun to sense a giggle going through her class every time she set the inevitable 'How I spent my school holidays' as the vacation task. This time they were going to get a surprise:

'is "How I spent the last day of my holidays."'

She was disappointed, because she sensed an identical giggle going around the class. She frowned like a disappointed fish, her protuberant eyes glaring through the rimless spectacles until she noticed that Morgan Fairclough was already setting down the odd note on a piece of rough paper. She did not ask herself how Morgan could be making notes for an essay on the last day of his holidays when the holiday had not yet begun. She approved of Morgan: solid and hard-working, though these virtues were tinged with arrogance when he talked to his less gifted classmates. But his estimable qualities were so much better than brilliance or flair that she looked forward to reading his account.

Morgan began his account two days after the day in question. He knew it was going to be hard to get the facts and angle right. He was after all the son of a writer. And he had to use mostly fact. There were still so many around who knew the facts: Mum, Deirdre, Timothy, Samantha . . .

Morgan licked the point of his Uniball and began.

HOW I SPENT THE LAST DAY OF MY HOLIDAYS

Morgan Fairclough, aged 11.

Please excuse all spelling mistakes. My dad has not tought me to use a dictionery as he promised to do in the holidays.

While she was clearing away breakfast things my mum said: 'Are you planning to have one almighty row over lunch, or would you prefer this time to have a series of minor explosions going off throughout the day?'

My father stretched, smiling a narsty smile.

'I think the latter, all things considered. Or maybe it would be fun to have no row at all. Have them waiting nervously all the time for something that never comes.'

'Oh, very suttle,' said my mother. 'Anyone would think they were not family but enemies.'

'Can't they be both? I must say that's how I regard them.'

All this I'd heard over and over in previous years. By

now it sounded rehearsed, like a play. One of my dad's plays. Rows were an everyday occurrence in our house, and the terms of the rows never really altered.

'You only regard them as enemies because they're my family,' said my mum.

'They can be your family and still be your enemies,' said Dad. 'In fact I remember when you and I were courting, you and Deirdre were constantly at each other's throats. Both of you were feisty girls after all.'

'Now you're being ridiculous,' said Mum. 'Of course I love Deirdre, and did then.'

But I noticed Mum disappeared into the kitchen and began the washing up. Running away from a fight – that's how I saw it.

'Anyway,' said my mother ten minutes later, coming back with her arms white from soapsuds, 'after all these yearly rows they won't come expecting a good time.'

'I don't know why we don't stop asking them,' said Dad. 'They don't ask us to Greenacre Manor. Probably afraid we'll use the wrong knives and forks.'

Deirdre's husband Timothy had sold his father's car hire companies when he inherited them and bought into traditional bricks and mortar, playing the squire to the point of ridiculousness (these are my dad's words – he can be very spiteful). Uncle Timothy is Head of Religious Broadcasting at the BBC. Dad says his religion is tweed suiting, pipe-smoking and *Brideshead Revisited*.

'I think you're right,' said Mum. 'Just make a row big enough to justify it and I'll put my oar in and suggest we call it a day. It will follow naturally if we do that.'

'Hmmm. Not a bad idea,' said Dad. But I could tell he was having second thoughts about his proposal. He always gave the impression of enjoying himself in these annual rows, and I must admit I thought they were quite fun.

'I like Uncle Timothy,' I said. 'Some of the things he says make me laugh.'

'They make me laugh too,' said Dad. 'Like his pretending to be still in love with Deirdre after all this time.'

'So the row is still on the schedule,' said my mother. 'Is after the walk the best time for staging it? Because that's what it is: a little play, stored away for when, if ever, you write your own *Who's Afraid of Virginia Wolf*.'

'If that's what I'm aiming for the rows would have to be with you, Lois.'

'Well, God knows, you've had enough experience of them. Oh shit – that's them now.'

My father cast an eye at the window, the Rolls outside, and the path that led from the front gate.

'Oh, God Almighty!'

For a household containing not one Believer we were very free with God's name. When I wrenched my eyes away from Auntie Deirdre, who looked as if she was carrying a shopping basket in front of her under her dress, I caught a look on Dad's face that was a mixture of relish and foreknowledge. He'd known in advance!

Exclamations took up the first two minutes of the visit.

'Well, this is a surprise!'

'Exactly what it was to us too.'

'How far are you gone, Deirdre?'

'Do you know what it is?'

'Samantha, are you looking forward to having a brother or sister?'

This welcome on the front door mat was quite convincing. It was led by my dad, who, being a playwrite of sorts, knew what people tended to say on all kinds of occasions. Mum hugged her sister, perhaps to hide the horrid display of jealousy on her face. Whatever Deirdre had Mum had to be jealous of, even if she would have died rather than be pregnant again.

'No, we weren't "trying" as they say,' said Deirdre, her voice high and a bit strident, 'and yes we are delighted, the feetus is five months old, we're doing all the right things that doctors and nurses recommend. All right? Sensation over?'

And she steamed ahead into the sitting room as if her shopping basket gave her all the rights of the lady of the house. There was a sparkle in her eye that suggested that she, like me, had something up her sleeve.

'Tim? what will you have?' gushed my father. 'And Deirdre, what can you have?'

'I'll risk a gin and tonic,' said Uncle Timothy. 'We go on the principle of "one off, all off" in our household, but I'm on leave at the moment. Deirdre will have pineapple juice, won't you, darling?'

'Yes, darling, and so will you. The fact that we are away from our own household doesn't let you off the "no alcohol" regimen.'

Timothy sighed.

'I would swear if the children weren't here. All my

abstention valued as nothing if I have one little lapse.'

'Go away, children,' said Dad, waving an artistic hand towards the garden. 'Your uncle doesn't like being found out, Morgan.'

When we got outside in the hallway I put my finger to my lips and we listened for a minute or two to the conversation.

'So, then, you're happy are you?' my father asked. 'Not just putting a brave face on a nasty accident?'

'We're over the moon! We talk baby talk all the time, and discuss colours for the nursery. We're even more delighted than Samantha.'

'Maybe she's too old to be totally pleased. At three – yes. At thirteen – no. They feel they'll degenerate into the resident babysitter.'

'I didn't realise you knew so much about growing families, Bernard.'

'I have a creative writer's understanding of how people think and feel, Timothy.'

Same old dialogue. Dad as a scriptwriter ought to have been able to think up something better, or at least different. Samantha and I shook our heads and moved over towards the kitchen door, where Aunt Deirdre and Lois my mum were well away.

'I'm not going to pretend it didn't come as a shock,' said Auntie D. 'We didn't take out all our old Noddy books and Paddington Bears and look forward to reading them at bedtimes over and over again. But when all is said, Catholics are right about abortion. It is murder, and just thinking about it we *felt* like murderers. I've settled down to all the rules and the deprivations . . . This martini is heaven, though.'

'You're a bit mean not letting Tim off his oath of abstention, I feel.'

'Timothy has nothing to complain of. Do you think he hasn't got a stash of booze somewhere in the house, if only I could find it? . . . But really, sis, you ought to try a late pregnancy.'

'I can't think of a single reason why I should.'

'You wouldn't believe how *different* pregnancy is in the twenty-first century. And almost always for the better. We had Morgan and Samantha at pretty much the same time, didn't we?'

'Yes, we did. Almost as if there was some kind of competition.'

Deirdre waved away the suggestion with a well-manicured hand.

'Oh, we were silly about some things then. But pregnancy is not what it was – it's easier, more straightforward. I tell you: you should try it.'

'Not on your life,' said Mum.

'Don't you dare!' I shouted.

'Morgan – vamoose,' called Mum. 'This is girls' talk.'

We didn't vamoose, and they started up again immediately. I waited until I was sick of the anatomical details (many of which I knew already), and then I made off towards the garden. I was rather surprised (because I count her even lower than the earthworm) when Samantha followed me. She started in on why she had come out – she felt in a position to give advice.

'Don't let my mum persuade yours to have another baby,' she said.

'She won't,' I said dismissively. 'I was more than enough for her.'

'I was quite pleased at first. Not delighted, but quite pleased. Then I thought that this is the age when I should be getting more freedom. What shall I get in fact?'

'Twenty-four hour slavery.'

'Right. Unpaid babysitter. Changing nappies non-stop. They're indescribably smelly and nasty, including the instantly disposable ones. I know she'll be poohing the whole time.'

'She?'

'Mummy pretends to Daddy that she doesn't know, but she does. It's a she. And Daddy does desperately want a son and heir. Greenacre Manor will be as dust and ashes without someone to inherit it – and of course to Daddy that means a male. He's often said he'd like to adopt you.'

I pricked up my ears.

'You're joking of course. He hardly notices me.'

'He notices. If he had his way you would be son and heir.'

I considered this.

'Your daddy's not that rich. It wouldn't be worth my while. I've never really considered him when I've dreamt about being adopted by a filthy-rich man or woman.'

'Daddy is high up in the BBC. The BBC is run by families. Dinnersties they call them: the Magnusens, the Dimblebies, the Michelmores. Being a child of a BBC person is a passport to a good, cushy job, well-paid and with lots of presteege. And jobs for your kids as well.'

'He's got you. Why should he need a son?'

'He's horribly old-fashioned.'

'Well, England has had queens since fifteen fifty-something. You'd think even Uncle Timothy could have got used to the idea by now . . .'

'He did once condesend to ask me if I wanted to work at the BBC.'

'What did you say?'

'I said I wanted to do a degree in the History of Western Art, then go and work in the Queen's Gallery at Buck House.'

'Beats the corridors of the dear old Beeb.'

'It just occurred to me as he spoke. I'm going to keep all my options open, but those options certainly do not include the Beeb. I said: "Give the job to the newcomer, Daddy. He or she is probably thick as pigshit."'

'How interesting. Come on, that's Mum calling for lunch.'

'Oh God! Rack of lamb and tiramisu.'

I will slip quickly over what we had for lunch, apart from the lamb and the tiramisu. There was a lot about babies, a lot about the power structures and the behavioural disharmonies (their words) at the BBC, and quite a lot (from my dad, of course) about the creative urge, and how it needed to be stimulated, not crushed. After lunch Dad and Deirdre did the washing up while Tim and Lois talked in the living-room. Tim had a stiff tumbler of white wine concealed between his chair and the wall, and kept taking quick surreptitious gulps. Mum, for some reason, was asking whether he saw a big change in Dad, whether he looked older and whether the non-stop creativity (he'd had a half-hour play on Armchair Theatre on Radio Four in the last two years) wasn't taking it out of him. When Dad and Deirdre came back in they all four (juniors were not consulted) agreed on a brisk walk up to Trevelyan Cave, and they were just rugging up and putting on walking boots when Deirdre dropped her bombshell.

'Oh, I've been meaning to tell you since we arrived, but there hasn't been a convenient opening. In one of Bernard's plays there would have been one, but he just forgot to provide one for real life.'

'Deirdre—'

'So I'll just have to tell you at an *un*suitable moment. Bernard and I go back a long time as all of you know, and we have been meeting up again over the last six months. In grubby little hotel bedrooms hired by the hour. We were taking things up where we left them off twelve or thirteen years ago. This' (patting her stomach) 'is Bernard's. He'd quite like a daughter in place of that little know-all in short pants he has already. He thinks we are going to get married as soon as the divorce goes through. Think on, Bernard. Marriage has outlived its usefulness. As far as I'm concerned sex is a short-term affair, with plenty of swapping. So it's bye-bye Tim, bye-bye Bernard. And welcome anyone young, fit and into it for the laughs.'

And she left the room and the house with a merry wave of her hand. The two men hurried after her and Samantha followed *them*, and we passed all four a few minutes along Caves Pathway, arguing and jesticulating. Mum didn't honour them with so much as a glance. She and I were usually together on these walks because we are the slowest. This year we were in front, and well in front too.

'Are they coming?' Mum asked after a bit. I looked round.

'Yes, but quite slowly. They're still arguing.'

'They would be, wouldn't they? When is it any different on these reunion days? I could murder Bernard.'

'Well, we've come to the right place,' I said, but seriously, not waggish at all. 'Sheer drop at several points. Hardly a soul around.'

'True,' said my mother, also treating the question seriously. 'But murder is too good for him. I should leave him alive, to moulder in his horrible skin, with his horrible self and his awful little talent.'

'I think murder would be better.'

At this point in his writing Morgan laid down his pen. Had he overdone it in directing suspicion on himself? It was a common ploy in crime fiction he had read. Probably it mirrored reality – policemen are *really thick and do get it wrong, in all probability. If a reader took it too seriously he had only to read on to change his opinion.*

He took up his pen again.

'You're probably right,' said my mother. 'But do you think I'm the murdering type?'

'You're the Agatha Christie type: least likely suspect.'

'I'm not sure the police would take that line. I don't get the impression they read Christie.'

'It's about half an hour to Trevelyan's Cave. Sheer

drop from there. Half the suicides' bodies are never recovered.'

'Little monster. Have you been planning this? How did you know that?'

'The *South Devon Chronicle.*'

'Shame on them . . . I was telling the truth when I said I could murder him . . . Taking up with that whore, twelve years after he ditched her for me.'

'I thought she ditched him for Uncle Tim, and you got him instead.'

'No . . . Well, have it your own way if you like . . . To go back to her, have regular . . . meetings in gungy hotel rooms—'

'Sex. It's called sex, Mum.'

'I know, cheeky. Or I remember . . . Well, that's the end, murder or no murder – and I think I can restrain myself from slortering him.'

I was afraid that was true. But when we got to Trevelyan Cave I was relieved that she went into the dirty little hole and sat down among the rocks. I stood outside where I had a spectacular view of the deadly rocks on Westcot cove, and also of the path, winding its vert-something-or-other way up to the Cave. I was looking for a little party of four, but I soon saw I was mistaken: the party had broken up, with Deirdre, Tim and Samantha probably going back to the village and then back to their Manor home which one day may be mine. There was one solitary trousered figure trailing his way up to us. All he needed was a napsack on his back and he'd be one of your typical boring-as-hell walkers.

'Here comes Dad,' I said. Mum elbowed her way to the front of the cave and I took over the shadows. 'He's going to beg you to take him back,' I said, in case he did.

'He's got a nerve,' muttered my mother. But he didn't do anything of the sort.

'I'm not stopping,' he panted, in the misstatement of the century. 'I just wanted to say goodbye. You always knew Deirdre was the one, didn't you? You always knew I was imagining her when we were . . . you know. It makes me sound a jerk, I know.'

'Not just sound,' said Mum.

'All right, all right. But I'm going to win her back. I'm going to go to her. Tim knows he's lost her, and I'm not sure he'll care all that much. He's told me he always loved you, Morgan – Oh, like a father, you know. I told him to keep his hands off you because we don't want his bloody Brideshead—'

I shot out of the cave, and the sentence was only completed with an 'AAAAHHH'. When I was capable of taking my eyes away from the prospect at the bottom of the cliffs Lois was looking around – up, down, and towards the edge – with a gaze of total bewilderment on her face. I felt almost sorry for her.

'Congratulations, Mum. You did it.'

'But I didn't. I mean I can't remember that I . . . *Did* I? Morgan, DID I? Oh my God, I must have. What are we going to do?'

'Go home. Tell people Bernard's been called away.'

My mother put her hand to her face.

'Australia! He was thinking of going to Australia. He's

writing some material for Dame Edna.'

'*Was* writing,' I said. 'Of course the body might be found.'

'But nothing to connect him to us. It would be much more likely that he committed suicide, or just missed his footing. There's been no one on the path to say that he ever got as high as Trevelyan Cave.'

'And no one to say we were here. Come on, Mum: let's get back home. I think Dad's going to like Australia so much he's going to be there for a very long time.'

Morgan stopped writing. He wondered whether it was totally clear what he wanted the reader to think. Well – not totally clear: this was a literary exercise, but one which could result in his being parentless and ripe for adoption. For a literary exercise it was surely a lot more exciting than most.

When Morgan was called into Miss Trim's office he knew exactly what he was going to say. The end of his father had been to a degree 'impovised', as he called it, but the broad outlines had been with him (as a fantasy hardening to a project) for some time. He could cope with the likes of Miss Trim.

'I must say, Morgan, that your essay bewildered me, even shocked me.'

'Oh? Why was that Miss Trim?'

'I expected it to be a factual, that means truthful, account of what you did on the last day of your holiday.'

'You didn't say that, Miss Trim. And I expect you know that my father is an imaginative writer.'

'Well, your father wasn't—'

'He makes it up. I find it runs in the family. I get to a certain point and then my imagination takes over.'

'Ah!' It was a sigh of relief. 'So you made a little play out of your day, so to speak?'

'A little story, Miss Trim. A play would be all dialogue and stage directions. I hope you enjoyed the story.'

'Oh, I did,' said Miss Trim untruthfully. 'But of course it made me uneasy, since all the others were truthful accounts of their day.'

'They're not a very imaginative lot, 6A.'

'Tell me, Morgan, why did you decide to write a story in which your father got . . . well, killed?'

Morgan shrugged.

'Well, it's just one sort of story, isn't it? They call it a Whodunnit. You don't know till towards the end who did it. My father's never had much time for me. Oh, he's there if I need him, but he hopes and prays I don't need him too much. Same with my mother. He cares more about the characters in his piffling plays. He'll pack a few things and take off at the drop of a hat. You wouldn't know this, Miss Trim, because he never comes to parents' days or anything like that. Doesn't care.'

'Oh, I'm sure he does. Some people find emotional things very difficult. Well, I think that was all. You've cleared up things nicely. I think I'd better ring your mother in case she hears rumours – gossip from your classmates or their parents.'

'They wouldn't know fact from fiction,' said Morgan contemptuously. He got up and walked towards the

door. 'Thank you for being so understanding, Miss Trim.'

As he opened the door he saw her hand straying towards the telephone. His face was suffused by an expression of sublime self-congratulation. He stood outside the door, his ear close to it.

'Mrs Fairclough? Oh, it's Edith Trim, from Westward School. I've just been talking to Morgan, always a pleasure. Sophisticated without being, well, snooty with it. He's written this essay about the last days of the school holidays, and he turned it into a really promising little story – he must be reading Agatha Christie and writers like that . . . Oh, he is! I guessed well. Now, there's a murder of course, and it's quite intriguing and exciting, but I just wanted to tell you, in case rumours come back to you that he is writing gruesome stories which gave kids sleepless nights and all that. Parents tell all sorts of silly tales about any child who makes up stories. It's really not that sort of story at all . . . I hope you can make it to the next parents' evening, Mrs Fairclough. We could have a good talk. And do try to bring your husband. I know Morgan would appreciate his being there. Oh . . . Oh . . . Oh, Australia. I see. Well, I'm sorry. We'll hope to see him next term.'

Morgan heard the receiver being put down. He started walking along the corridor, the smug expression still suffusing his face. This was going to be one of those subgenre stories, in this case one of those in which the wrong suspect is fitted up for a murder he, or in fact she, didn't do. And it was going to be one in which the murderer is the one telling the story. Morgan was enormously pleased with himself for thinking of that. It was exceptionally clever, and something he was quite sure would never occur to a pedestrian mind like Agatha Christie's.

A Political Necessity

It must be rare for the first thought of a newly appointed government minister to be: Now is the time to kill my wife. Don't get me wrong – I'm sure many of my colleagues would like to, with that dull, insistent sort of wishing which will never actually impel them to action, and which is characteristic of second-rate minds. My thought was not 'If only I could' but 'Now I can'. It had my typical decisiveness and lack of sentiment, as well as that ability to get to the heart of a question and come up with a solution which I am sure was the reason the prime minister decided to promote me.

I was brought into the government in the autumn reshuffle, and my second thought was: Christmas is coming. Ideal.

I should explain that the post I was given was one of the junior positions in the Home Office. I doubt whether the thought would have occurred to me if it had been in Trade and Industry, or Environment. The Home Office, you see, has a great deal to do with Northern Ireland, and everything to do with the imprisonment of IRA terrorists. Its ministers, therefore, are natural targets. Indeed, two days after I took up my post, I had a visit by arrangement from a high-ranking Scotland Yard terrorist officer who lectured me on personal security; elementary precautions I and my family could take, and little indications that might give me the idea that something was wrong.

Including, naturally, suspect packages.

He actually brought along a mock-up suspect package, showed me all the signs that should arouse my suspicions, and then proceeded to take it apart and show me the sort of explosive device that would be concealed inside. It was a real education.

I tried not to show too much interest. Indeed, I hope I gave the impression of a man who is trying to give due attention to an important matter, but who has actually a mountain of things he ought to be doing. In fact my mind was ticking away as inexorably as a real explosive device. A suspect package among her Christmas parcels – a sort of *bombe surprise*. How wonderful if it could have gone off while she was singing 'Happy Birthday, dear Jesus' with the children. But of course that was out of the question. I had no particular desire to harm my children. Merely to render them motherless.

There are many reasons why the old custom of wife murder has not fallen into disuse in this age of easy – indeed practically obligatory – divorce. One is to get custody of the children. Another is money. Another is personal satisfaction that no divorce can give. My situation is peculiar. Normally even an MP can move out of the family home, make mutterings about 'irretrievable breakdown,' and in two shakes of a duck's tail be shacking up with his secretary, or Miss Bournemouth 1989, or whomever he has had his eye on. Not the MP for the constituency of Dundee Kirkside. My constituents, though Conservative almost to a man and woman, are tight-lipped, censorious, pleasure-hating accountants and small shopkeepers, people for whom John Knox did not go nearly far enough. Liquor never passes their lips, dance never animates their lower limbs – their very sperm is deep-frozen.

Divorce, for the MP for Dundee Kirkside, was a non-starter.

Equally, living for the rest of my life with Annabelle was simply not to be contemplated. If I had not known this before, I certainly knew it at a Downing Street dinner shortly after my appointment. As ill luck would have it, Annabelle was seated near to the prime minister, while I was someway down on the other side of the table. But of course I am all too attuned to her voice, and I heard her say, 'Whenever I see my two little ones tucked up in their little bed, I always seem to see the baby Jesus there making a third!'

The prime minister's face was a picture. So, I imagine, was mine.

Not that Annabelle's style of conversation, apparently derived from Victorian commonplace books designed to be given as Sunday school prizes, hadn't been useful to me in the past. I'd be the first to admit that in private. For instance, being only half-Scottish (and on my mother's side at that) and having been educated at Lancing, I was not an obvious candidate for a Scottish constituency. Thank God we Tories still interview the wives as part of the selection procedure! I don't say anyone was melted by Annabelle's liquid caramel smile, but they were enraptured by her expressed conviction that we (we in the Conservative party) are on this earth to do the Lord's bidding, that she prayed every night that her husband would do the Lord Jesus's work, that we were the party of the family, and the Christian family at that – and a lot more balls along these lines. I got the nomination, and we celebrated by going down on our knees beside the twin beds in our hideous Dundee hotel room. It was the least I could do. Luckily the curriculum vitae which I submitted to the selection committee had merely stated that we had been married in 1985 and our first child born in 1986 – months not given. Being the party of the family didn't mean they approved of women who were in the family way when they went to the altar.

That happened, of course, before Annabelle got religion from a poisonous American woman evangelist at a dreadful rally in Earls Court that she had gone along to under the impression that it was *Aida* with elephants.

'I'm so longing for Christmas to come this year,' burbled Annabelle, her eyes all fizzing sparklers. 'Just us and our two babies celebrating the coming of Jesus.'

I looked at her with love in my eyes and Semtex in my heart.

'It will be lovely. But, do you know, I sometimes regret the Christmases of my childhood. Over in Belgium the real celebration was Christmas Eve.'

My family retreated to Ostend, in the manner pioneered by bankrupt Victorians, when I was five. This was as a consequence of a disagreement my father had with the Inland Revenue which was not sorted out for many years. I have no idea whether the Belgians do in fact celebrate Christmas Eve. It was bad enough living with the clog-hoppers, without mixing with them. But I do know that many Continental countries do, and Annabelle has no knowledge of habits and customs outside Pinner.

'How odd,' she said in reply. 'Before the baby Jesus was actually born. I'm not sure I'd like that.'

'Don't be so parochial,' I said. 'God isn't just English. He's got the whole world in his hands, remember.'

That set Annabelle off singing for the rest of the evening in her clear, bright Julie Andrews voice that can shatter glass ornaments if she goes too high.

I, meanwhile, was not neglecting the practical side. I never do – it's part of my strength. I've always been pretty smart at do-it-yourself, and to explain my evening hours in the garage I told Annabelle that I was preparing a little surprise for Gavin and Janet at Christmas. Which wasn't so far from the truth. I had already made an incognito visit (luckily for me I am still so junior that my face is not known, which will not be the case for long) to Tottenham Court Road, where I picked up one of the devices the inspector had so kindly demonstrated to me. Fortunately I had a very dodgy contact in the underworld (I had used him when I worked for Conservative Central Office, for a small job of ballot-rigging), and from him I got the modest quantity of explosive necessary to send Annabelle into the arms of the Lord Jesus.

All was going beautifully to plan.

While all this was coming to fruition, I was naturally fulfilling – very energetically fulfilling – my obligations and duties at the Home Office. I was also making routine preparations for Christmas, or getting other people to do them for me. I paid particular attention to getting the right presents for Annabelle. I meant her to die happy – or, if she insisted on leaving my presents till later, I intended to make much, in a thoroughly maudlin way, of what pleasures I had had in store for her to the Special Branch officers who would investigate her death. I bought a diamond pendant from Cartier's; I had one of the bookish secretaries from the Home Office scouring the secondhand bookshops of Highgate and Hampstead for a copy of *The Bible Designed to Be Read as Literature*, which she had expressed a desire for – everything, right down to the Thornton's chocolates that she loved. Thoughtful presents, though I say so myself. The presents of a model husband.

The children's presents I could safely leave to her. She loved shopping for them, and she was usually out when I rang home in the weeks leading up to Christmas, on some spree or other of that kind. I got one of the secretaries to ring Harrods, and by the eighteenth a large Christmas tree was in place in the living room. Annabelle, the children, and the Norwegian au pair decorated it the same day. They were just finishing it when I arrived back from Whitehall.

'Do you celebrate Christmas Eve or Christmas Day in Norway?' I asked Margrethe.

'Christmas Eve,' she said promptly. 'That is when the Christmas gnome brings all the presents.'

I smiled at her more benevolently than usual and suppressed any comment about the Christmas gnome. Really, was it a Christian country or a European Disneyland?

'You know, I think we'll do that this year,' I said to Annabelle later than evening. 'Celebrate *our* Christmas on Christmas Eve, after the babies have gone to bed. Then we can give all our time and attention to them on Christmas Day itself. Their day, entirely and completely.'

'Perhaps you're right,' said Annabelle, smiling her melting-fudge smile. 'When you come to think about it, Christmas Day should be just for the little ones, shouldn't it?'

Soon the packages began to pile up under the tree. Presents from grandparents, aunties, presents from constituents, especially from businessmen and property developers anxious to keep on the right side of me. Most of them were for Gavin and Janet, of course, but Annabelle and I soon had a respectable number. I began to separate the piles – the children's on one side of the tree, ours on the other.

On December the twenty-first I put the suspect package into the pile – a brown padded envelope, with a stamp and a fake postmark. It nestled shyly under bigger and gaudier packages.

Christmas is a very uninteresting time in politics. Nothing important gets announced (unless it is something dodgy we are hoping to slip past the public with little publicity), and so many of the MPs slope off home early that there is very little of the cut and thrust of political infighting which is what I excel at. Even in the department things slackened off. I was able to get home on two or three afternoons in the lead-up period. I found Annabelle out shopping and the kids in the charge of Margrethe. Margrethe proved very unresponsive to my suggestions of how we should spend the afternoon. Really, Norwegians are not all they're cracked up to be.

Once she had got the idea of a special dinner for us on Christmas Eve, Annabelle chattered on about what it should be. The damned kids insisted on turkey on The Day, of course, though I can think of about twenty meats I would find more interesting. We finally decided on a cold meal – light, but with a few touches of luxury. Margrethe was flying back to Bergen on the twenty-third, but she did some of the preparations before she went. We really get quite a lot of work out of Margrethe. I made one or two suggestions – not that I expected to eat anything much, but in order that it should look right to the investigating officers. I would have been a superb stage director. Annabelle said she could get some of the things at the delicatessen around the corner, and she would get the rest at Harrods. She also said it was going to be an absolutely smashing evening.

The day dawned. The children ('the babies,' as Annabelle calls them, though they are no longer that, thank God) were of course wild with pre-Christmas excitement, so I escaped to the office for most of the day. There was, after all, nothing left to do. Soon after I got home I suggested it was time for the kids to go to bed, and as they were confidently expecting a visit from Santa Claus, they didn't make too many objections. Then I began setting the scene. I put the drinks on the phone table at the far end by the door.

I intended to be over there when Annabelle opened the package. I toyed with the idea of being rather closer, to get the odd cut and scar from the debris, but I rejected the idea. Annabelle began bringing on the cold collation with a series of appreciative shrieks – 'Doesn't this look *scrumptious*?' and the like. The room was beautifully warm from the central heating, and I rejected Annabelle's suggestion that I light the fire. In fact, I was feeling distinctly sweaty, and I would have taken off my jacket and tie, except that I hate that sort of slovenliness. Round about seven-thirty, I said:

'I think it's about time for a drink.'

'Oh, goody!' said Annabelle. Getting God had not quenched her taste for dry martinis. I got her a large one with plenty of ice. Then I got for myself a gin and tonic that was mostly tonic and ice. Keep cool, George, keep cool!

'Now!' I said, and we looked at each other and smiled. We had agreed to open presents when we had our first drinks.

First of all we opened our own to each other. Annabelle oohed over the Cartier pendant ('You *shouldn't* have, Georgie boy! What must it have cost?') I tried to look pleased with a very expensive shaving kit.

'I really thought you should start shaving *properly*, Georgie. Electric razors are frightfully *infra*, and people are starting to comment on your midnight shadow. Look what harm that did to Richard Nixon.'

I regarded my midnight shadow as part of my saturnine and macho image. Nobody ever found Richard Nixon macho.

'I promise, my darling,' I said.

Then she opened her *Bible Designed to Be Read as Literature.*

'Oh, wonderful! How *thoughtful* you are, Georgie-Porgy. People say that reading this is an entirely new experience!' She opened it and read: '"There were shepherds abiding in the fields, keeping watch over their flocks by night."'

I suppose I was lucky she didn't sing it. She sometimes takes part in those come-along-and-sing Messiahs which are so very matey and democratic – practically the Labour Party at song. I opened a little square box and found a three-disc set of Luciano Pavarotti's greatest hits. Talk about things being *infra!* 'Perfect!' I said.

So we worked through our presents, eating chocolates and trying things on till at last she laid her hand on the brown padded envelope and took it up.

'What *is* this one?' she said.

My heart stood still. I tried with all the nonchalance my sweaty state would allow to take up one of my presents and open it.

'Haven't the faintest idea.'

'I noticed it the other day. Did it really come by post?'

'How would I know?'

'Because neither Margrethe nor I took it in, so you must have done.'

'Can't remember. I may have done, I suppose.'

'If so, it must have been Sunday. It's the only day when you were on your own here. I didn't think they delivered parcels on Sunday. What did the postman look like?'

Normally this would have been a cue for a spurt of sarcasm on my part. I hoped Annabelle would attribute it to the Christmas spirit that it was not forthcoming.

'Good heavens, one doesn't notice what postmen look like,' I said mildly. 'If you're wondering who sent it, you'd better open it and find out.'

She was looking at it closely.

'The postmark is all smudged. In fact it doesn't look like a real postmark at all.' She got up. 'Georgie, I think we ought to phone the police.'

She walked over toward the phone. I felt my face going red; our positions in my plan were exactly reversed. I forced myself to take up the package.

'Of course I see what you're getting at, darling, but I really do think that you're panicking needlessly. I don't see any of the things the inspector said should put us on our guard. It's not from Ireland, the name is spelled right – there are none of the signs. A smudged postmark is hardly unusual.'

Her finger was poised over the press-button dial. 'Better safe than sorry.'

'No!'

My voice had come out very loud. The police would almost certainly be able to trace the package back to me if they got it intact. Annabelle paused.

'No?'

'I mean . . . we'd look awful fools . . . disturbing them on Christmas Eve, for nothing.'

'How unusually considerate of you, Georgie. But you've been unusual for quite a while now. I'm beginning to think that Paul is right.'

'Paul?'

'A chap I've been seeing.'

'Seeing?'

'He said that if I drove you too mad with my Pollyanna act, it wouldn't be divorce I drove you to but murder. He's seen you on television from the House. He thinks you're mad.'

'Annabelle, look, this really has gone too far. There's no need at all to call the police. I was told all about suspect packages. This one hasn't got the look of one at all.'

She stood there, twenty feet away from me, her hand poised over the dial, very, very cool.

'All right, buster: open it.'